The Forger's Wife

JOHN LANG

with an introduction by KEN GELDER *and* RACHAEL WEAVER,
and an appendix translated by SOPHIE ZINS

Grattan Street Press

ABOUT THE AUSTRALIAN CENTRE

The Australian Centre is based in the School of Culture and Communication at the University of Melbourne, with Professor Ken Gelder and Professor Denise Varney as its co-directors. It aims to develop innovative research projects in the Australian arts and humanities across a range of disciplines, including Art History, Theatre Studies, Literary Studies, Cultural Studies, Media and Communication, Cinema Studies, Indigenous Studies and Creative Writing.

Grattan Street Press is the imprint of the
teaching press based in the School of Culture
and Communication at the University of
Melbourne, Parkville, Australia.

THE UNIVERSITY OF
MELBOURNE

The Forger's Wife originally published in serial form in *Fraser's Magazine* in 1853,
as 'Emily Orford'.
The Forger's Wife was first published in book form in 1855.

Grattan Street Press
School of Culture and Communication
John Medley Building,
Parkville, VIC 3010
www.grattanstreetpress.com

Printed in Australia

National Library of Australia Cataloguing-in-Publication entry

Title: The forger's wife / John Lang ; Ken Gelder ; Rachael Weaver; Sophie Zins.
ISBN: 9780987625304 (paperback)
Series: Colonial Australian popular fiction ; Vol. 1.
Notes: Includes bibliographical references.
Subjects: Detective and mystery stories.
Sydney (N.S.W.)--Fiction.
Other Creators/Contributors:
Gelder, Ken D., editor, writer of introduction.
Weaver, Rachael, editor, writer of introduction.
Zins, Sophie, translator.

CONTENTS

SERIES INTRODUCTION

The Colonial Australian Popular Fiction series brings the excitement and diversity of colonial Australian fiction to the attention of contemporary readers – and there is certainly some remarkable fiction to read here.

Encompassing both novels and short-story collections, the series will include a range of popular genres that flourished during the colonial period: the bush sketch, the Lemurian novel, crime and detective fiction, the colonial romance, the Gothic tale, the convict novel, the goldfields adventure and the bushranger novel. Some of the authors were bestsellers in their day, and their work can still take us by surprise. We aim to make colonial Australian fiction accessible to contemporary readers – and we hope the design and layout of these works will be helpful here. But we also want to honour the original forms of these works. So we have reprinted from first editions or from the original serialisation of a work in newspapers or journals. Each publication includes a short introduction written by academic specialists, which provides a brief biography of the author (or authors) and offers critical insight into the work and its contexts. We would be particularly pleased if some of our publications become set texts in university or senior secondary courses. We believe that all readers have much to gain from these vibrant works from our turbulent colonial past.

The Colonial Australian Popular Fiction series is an ongoing collaboration between Grattan Street Press and the Australian Centre, both based within the School of Culture and Communication at the University of Melbourne.

INTRODUCTION
Ken Gelder and Rachael Weaver

John George Lang was Australia's first locally born novelist. His grandfather, John Harris, was a transported convict who arrived with the First Fleet in 1788; Harris was later emancipated and was instrumental in the establishment of a night watch police system in Sydney and later on Norfolk Island. In 1812, Harris's daughter Elizabeth married a Scottish sea captain, Walter Lang, who died of a long illness only a few years later on 30 March 1816. John Lang was their second son, born in Parramatta in December of that year. Elizabeth remarried three years later to the prosperous merchant, sealer and trader, Joseph Underwood. As Rick Hosking notes, John Lang 'grew up in a wealthy household that had strong connections with India and in particular with Calcutta'.[1]

Lang was educated in Sydney, winning a gold medal at Sydney College 'in approbation of his talents, acquirements, and general good conduct'.[2] He went on to study law at Cambridge but was 'sent down' early on for some misdemeanour, completing his degree at Middle Temple in London. In October 1841, Lang returned to Sydney with his wife, Lucy, and a young daughter, and began a career as a barrister. His temperament may have been unsuited to

1   Hosking, Rick. 'Preface: Who was John Lang?'. In *Wanderings in India: Australian Perceptions*, edited by Rick Hosking and Amit Sarwal. Clayton: Monash University Publishing, 2012. http://books.publishing.monash.edu/apps/bookworm/view/Wanderings+in+India%3A+Australian+Perceptions/178/OEBPS/pre.htm.

2   Cited in Nancy Keesing, *John Lang & "The Forger's Wife": A True Tale of Early Australia* (Sydney: John Ferguson, 1979), p.35.

the job. Victor Crittenden talks about Lang's 'propensity to dive into controversy' and his 'larrikin attitude',[3] suggesting his argumentative manner may not have helped his reputation as a member of the Australian Patriotic Association, an organisation founded by the conservative New South Wales politician William Charles Wentworth. Wentworth even gets a brief mention in *The Forger's Wife*. Lang was also writing fiction by this time. Crittenden wonders if Lang was the author of the bestselling 1836 novel *Violet the Danseuse;* he also regards Lang as the author of a novella called *Raymond*, about a struggling translator, student and husband in Cambridge, published in *Blackwood's Edinburgh Magazine* in December 1840.[4] Lang had almost certainly begun writing fiction set in Australia while in Sydney. One or two stories were published locally in 1842 by James Tegg under the title *Legends of Australia*, but the series didn't last. By then, in any case, Lang and his family had left Sydney for Calcutta.

Lang practised law in India, although he struggled to make a living in the early years. His wife left him a few years after their arrival, taking their children with her to England. In 1845, Lang established a successful newspaper in Calcutta, the *Mofussilite*: the first issue in August included his 'A Ghost Story', which later appeared in revised form as 'The Ghost on the Rail' in Dickens's

3 Victor Crittenden, *John Lang: Australia's Larrikin Writer* (Canberra: The Mulini Press, 2005), pp.56, 57.

4 See Crittenden, *John Lang*, pp.2, 23, 36. Lang's translation of Horace's First Satire was published in Sydney in 1835; in *Raymond*, the protagonist tries to publish his translation of the plays of Aeschylus. Crittenden regards *Raymond* as an autobiographical novel. But by the end of the novel, Raymond's wife has died in childbirth and the protagonist commits suicide in despair. The *Wellesley Index to Victorian Periodicals, 1824 - 1900*, lists the author of *Raymond* as William Frederick Deacon, not John Lang.

Household Words.[5] Stephen Knight writes that 'If ghosts can be accepted as detectives...then ["The Ghost on the Rail"] is...Australia's first detective story'.[6] Lang eventually rose to prominence in India as a lawyer, taking on the East India Company and defending a celebrated Indian nationalist, Lakshmibai, the Rani of Jhansi, who went on to become a prominent activist in the 1857 Indian Mutiny. In 1853, Lang left India and went to live in England, where he further developed his literary career. His novel *Lucy Cooper: An Australian Tale* had already been serialised in *Sharpe's London Magazine* in 1846, and his much-reprinted *Too Clever by Half, or, The Harroways* was serialised in the *Mofussilite* in 1847 and 1848. It was first published as a novel by Nathaniel Cooke in London in 1853. This was the same year that Lang serialised *The Forger's Wife* in the influential London periodical *Fraser's Magazine of Town and Country*, under the original title 'Emily Orford'. Two years later, in 1855, *The Forger's Wife* was published as a novel by London's Ward and Lock, and has since been reprinted many times over.

It is generally accepted that *The Forger's Wife* is the first novel by an Australian-born novelist to feature an Australian detective. We also think it is the first detective novel in the Anglophone world. The first detective novel in English is usually taken to be *The Notting Hill Mystery*, written under the pseudonym 'Charles Felix' (possibly Charles Warren

---

5 Crittenden notes that the *Mofussilite's* 'A Ghost Story' was in fact already a 'retelling' of a story with the same title published in *Tegg's Monthly Magazine* in 1836: see Crittenden, *John Lang*, p.89.

6 Stephen Knight, *Continent of Mystery: A Thematic History of Australian Crime Fiction* (Melbourne: Melbourne University Press, 1997), p.20.

Adams);[7] but since that novel was serialised in 1862–1863, *The Forger's Wife* (as *Emily Orford*) predates it by about ten years. *Emily Orford*'s serialisation is in fact more or less contemporaneous with the serialisation of Dickens's *Bleak House* (1852–1853), which gives us the 'first fully developed police detective to feature in a novel',[8] a character called Mr. Bucket. But although Mr. Bucket is a perceptive and insightful figure, he appears only occasionally in *Bleak House*, later fading out of the novel altogether. In contrast, *The Forger's Wife* introduces a detective relatively early on who, almost literally, takes charge of the narrative. George Flower is a detective with the Sydney police, already well known, powerful and influential – 'a great character in the colony of New South Wales', as the novel puts it when it introduces him at the beginning of Chapter XI. Unlike Bucket, Flower stays with the novel right to the end and significantly shapes its outcomes. He is a major figure, a charismatic, enterprising character positioned right at the centre of events: the first detective-protagonist in an Anglophone novel.

The Forger's Wife begins by introducing Emily Orford, the privileged daughter of a British army officer who – after the attentions of many gentlemen suitors – finally elopes with the duplicitous Charles Roberts (*alias* Reginald Harcourt). Roberts is later accused of forgery and transported to Sydney Cove and Emily determines

---

7 Kate Watson attributes the claim that *The Notting Hill Mystery* is the 'first full-blown detective novel in English' to various literary commentators, including Stephen Knight, Julian Symons and Michael Cox: see *Women Writing Crime Fiction, 1860-1880: Fourteen American, British and Australian Authors* (Jefferson: McFarland & Company, Inc., 2012), p.18.

8 Watson, *Women Writing Crime Fiction*, p.18.

to follow him. The novel is a melodrama that follows the fairly familiar pattern of a female emigrant's tale – much like the actual forger Henry Savery's earlier novel *Quintus Servinton* (1830, 1832), which also tells of a woman who follows her convicted husband out to the colonies. When she arrives in Sydney, Emily finds herself in the midst of a tough, competitive colonial society full of characters on the make. Dominating this strange metropolitan frontier is the detective George Flower – another transported convict who (rather like Lang's grandfather) transitions into an effective local agent of the law. The problem here is to do with how much license the detective claims for himself in the midst of a colonial system where the law is already at breaking point. 'I can do anything I like in this country', Flower brags to Emily at one point; 'They say I am the greatest man in this large island, and I believe I am…There's nothing that I can't do'. This detective polices the colonial economy, but he also profits from it: stealing goods from criminals and beating them up in their cells (Roberts is 'leisurely thrashed'), ushering in the figure of the violent detective-who-pushes-the-boundaries so familiar in later Australian crime fiction. Flower is also a detective who relishes what he does and has fun with it. For such an early example of his character type, he is remarkably recognisable. He is unrelenting in his pursuit of criminals and accomplished in his methods of tracking them down – already a fully formed detective at the height of his powers. He is also a moralist, sentimental about the protection of wronged women, and espouses an honourable, vigorous model of masculinity. This is shown, for example, through his affection for the bushranger Millighan; by contrast, Flower has only contempt for what he sees as the unmanliness of Roberts, which is played up in the novel when, at one point, Roberts takes obvious pleasure dressing in women's clothes ('this whim of his lasted all night…he did not divest himself of the female attire until daylight next morning'). For a man who takes so many liberties with the colonial system, Flower is nevertheless determined to raise the standard of local conditions. This is a detective who is also committed to nation building. 'I wish to teach you settlers, and the Gov'ment…a great moral lesson', he tells a local squatter, Major Grimes. 'I want to make you more independent and secure – bushrangers less numerous and daring – and Gov'ment more economical and sensible'.

It is generally agreed that Flower's character was based on the actual figure of Israel Chapman, another transported convict who went on to become one of Sydney's most famous policemen. Nancy Keesing writes, 'Israel Chapman had an extraordinary career in the police force; he was notably strong, brave and resourceful and, in 1827, the situation of police runner, at a salary of £100 a year, was created for him in the police establishment… on the model of the famous Bow Street runners, who were, in effect, detectives'.[9] Keesing speculates that John Lang and Chapman may even have known each other because of their shared Jewish backgrounds. Flower, on the other hand, is presented as a fully-fledged 'colonial', completely embodying (even in his 'parlance') his antipodean predicament. *The Forger's Wife* follows Flower's career all the way to retirement, although even here he continues his detective work by trying to resolve a series of loose

9 Keesing, *John Lang & "The Forger's Wife"*, p.84.

ends. One of the many fascinating details that the novel leaves us with is a whimsical manifestation of Flower's colonial identity and a reversal of his own experience of transportation, when he sends a menagerie of 'Australian curiosities' ('kangaroos, emus, flying squirrels, parrots and cockatoos') back to his friends in England.

KEN GELDER is Professor of English and co-Director of the Australian Centre at the University of Melbourne.

RACHAEL WEAVER is an ARC Senior Research Fellow in English at the Australian Centre at the University of Melbourne.

WORKS CITED

Crittenden, Victor. *John Lang: Australia's Larrikin Writer.* Canberra: The Mulini Press, 2005.

Hosking, Rick. 'Preface: Who was John Lang?'. In *Wanderings in India: Australian Perceptions*, edited by Rick Hosking and Amit Sarwal. Clayton: Monash University Publishing, 2012. http://books.publishing. monash.edu/apps/bookworm/view/Wanderings+in+India%3A+Austr alian+Perceptions/178/OEBPS/pre.htm.

Keesing, Nancy. *John Lang and 'The Forger's Wife': A True Tale of Early Australia.* Sydney: John Ferguson, 1979.

Knight, Stephen. *Continent of Mystery: A Thematic History of Australian Crime Fiction.* Melbourne: Melbourne University Press, 1997.

Watson, Kate. *Women Writing Crime Fiction, 1860-1880: Fourteen America, British and Australian Authors.* Jefferson, N.C.: MacFarland & Company, Inc., 2012.

A NOTE ON THE TEXT

This edition of John Lang's *The Forger's Wife* follows the first edition of the novel, published in 1855 by Ward and Lock, 158 Fleet Street, London. *The Forger's Wife* was first serialised under the title *Emily Orford* in *Fraser's Magazine of Town and Country* over five volumes in the latter part of 1853: July (chapters 1–8: pp.98–114), August (chapters 9–18: pp.220–233), September (chapters 19–23: pp.326–341), October (chapters 24–29: pp.401–416) and December (chapters 30–37: pp.659–670). *Emily Orford* has 37 chapters, while *The Forger's Wife* has 40 chapters. This is because some of the chapters have been distributed differently rather than because of any major textual changes. A number of short descriptive passages (mostly brief paragraphs or single sentences) have been removed from the serialised version.

The Forger's Wife went through a number of subsequent serialisations in a range of regional and metropolitan newspapers, for example, Sydney's *Evening News* (April–June 1875) and Bathurst's *National Advocate* (August–October 1890, under the title *Assigned to His Wife*; and March–April 1896, under the title *Emily's Sacrifice*). The novel itself was reprinted many times over by Ward and Lock; it was also published in novel form by W. Tegg & Co. (1859), Melbourne's E.W. Cole and Hobart's J. Walch (1900), and the New South Wales Bookstall Company (n.d.) under the title *Assigned to His Wife; Or, The Adventures of George Flower, the Celebrated Detective Officer*.

We have included an image of the 1855 Ward and Lock cover on page 3.

We have also provided an English translation of the 'short tale' from the *Echo de Bruxelles* that Lang mentions in his 'Author's Preface' to the first edition of the novel.

The editors of the present text have sought to balance scholarly accuracy with readability. Some punctuation, capitalisation and hyphenation have been changed for the sake of consistency (e.g. 'George-Street' becomes 'George Street'). Scholars seeking an unamended text of this edition should contact us on info@grattanstreetpress.com for details.

The Forger's Wife

THE FORGER'S WIFE

BY JOHN LANG

AUTHOR OF

TOO CLEVER BY HALF

LONDON : WARD & LOCK, 158 FLEET ST.—ONE SHILLING.

AUTHOR'S PREFACE

The conductors of several German and French papers paid the author of this story the compliment of selecting it for translation and insertion in their columns, during its continuance in the columns of *Frazer's Magazine*; one of them, the *Echo de Bruxelles*, supplied a short tale, by way of episode, which will be found at the conclusion of this reprint.

It may not be out of place to mention that the story of *The Forger's Wife* is not a fiction; albeit the incidents are sufficiently disguised to spare the feelings of any surviving member of the family (called in the following pages 'Orford'). The letters written by the unfortunate lady, from New South Wales, came into the possession of the author some sixteen years ago, and it was from these letters (some of them dated 'Moreton Bay!') that the idea of her sufferings was gleaned.

Vienna, 22nd Jan., 1855.

CHAPTER I

I N ONE OF the midland counties, some years ago, there lived a gentleman of ancient family and large estate – a Mr. Orford, who had married, early in life, a young lady of great personal attractions, the daughter of a distinguished general officer in the British army.

The issue of this marriage was numerous, but one child only was reared – a girl. Some had died very young, others had lingered on till they were six or seven years of age, and two had been taken away – boy and a girl – when the former was fifteen and the latter fourteen.

With what anxiety did Mr. and Mrs. Orford watch Emily, their only child! Her every look was studied, every whim gratified, every want anticipated; and year by year did their anxiety become more intense.

When Emily had completed her thirteenth year, Mr. Orford, who represented his county, resigned his seat in Parliament, and removed his family to the Continent. For four years and upwards the Orfords remained abroad, travelling; and when they returned to England, Emily was seventeen years of age.

Emily was very pretty, and had remarkably pleasing manners. Her form was slight, her figure well-shaped and graceful. The sweetness of her disposition might be seen in her soft hazel eyes, the expression of her delicately formed mouth, and the intonations of her musical and unaffected voice. She was the beau ideal of a girl of gentle blood, and heiress to all her father possessed – a very considerable fortune, not less than fifteen thousand a year.

Amongst the many eligible suitors who visited at Orford Hall was a handsome, manly person – one Charles Everest, the second son of a baronet whose estate joined that of Emily's father.

For a year Charles Everest continued to pay Miss Orford the most 'marked' attention, which she received seemingly with delight. At length he proposed to her; but, to the disappointment of all who were interested in the matter, she refused to become his wife, though she acknowledged she liked him extremely. Charles Everest, dejected and abashed, removed himself from Emily's vicinity, and proceeded to London, where his father's interest soon procured for him an appointment – that of private secretary to a Cabinet Minister.

The next person whose attentions seemed far from disagreeable to Miss Orford was a Mr. Hastings, a young barrister in whose 'circuit' Mr. Orford's estate was situated. Mr. Hastings was 'a very rising man', and Mr. Orford, who was chairman of the Quarter Sessions, would frequently invite him to the Hall.

Mr. Orford was about to stand once more for the county, which he had formerly represented in Parliament, and his friend the barrister volunteered to canvass for him. The offer was accepted, and on this occasion the barrister remained for a fortnight under the same roof with Emily, with whom he became passionately in love.

Through the exertions of Mr. Hastings, Mr. Orford was returned by a very large majority; and Emily naturally shared her father's joy on this event. Her lover observing this, made a declaration of his attachment in the most eloquent terms. But it is one thing to move a jury or a mob by figures of speech and impassioned discourse – it is another thing to create that strange mysterious feeling, called 'love', in a maiden's breast. Emily owned that she liked Mr. Hastings, just as she had liked Charles Everest; but then she added, 'I could never think of marrying him, because I do not love him.'

~

Miss Orford's third suitor was an officer in the Coldstream Guards, Captain Deesing. He first saw Emily at a county ball, to which he had escorted his sisters. Deesing was a man for whom half the girls in London were breaking their hearts, contrary to the wishes of their mothers, for Deesing was in debt, and had no 'expectations'. Deesing's address was peculiarly captivating, and he had always at command a stock of fresh and entertaining pleasantries wherewith to amuse those with whom he entered into conversation. He could not only engage the affections of the fair sex with wonderful facility, but even men who had once spoken to him, long after thirsted for his society. Witty, clever, shrewd, good-tempered, frank, generous, unaffected, Deesing's smiles were courted by persons of all ranks. He had never thought of marriage; at least, he had thought that matrimony was not exactly suited to him, and therefore he had no idea of contracting it.

Captain Deesing was no sooner introduced to Miss Orford than he conceived for her a regard which he had never felt for any other woman; and the morning after the ball he communicated to his eldest sister that he was in love with her friend.

~

Although Captain Deesing saw Emily Orford almost every day for three weeks – although he had played in a charade with her, wherein they were ardent lovers – although his sisters had been loud in his praises – although he had escorted her in her morning rides, had walked with her alone in the shrubberies, had read poetry to her, had sang to her the tenderest songs; although he had striven hard, by exercising all his powers of fascination, to win her love; still, when he proposed to her, she told him what she had told the others, she liked him very much, but she could never think of marrying him.

This was a severe blow to Captain Deesing. He went to town; rejoined his regiment in disgust; shortly afterwards married a rich widow, and exchanged into a regiment of the line.

CHAPTER II

M RS. ORFORD WAS induced to visit a watering-
place in Devonshire. Mr. Orford's parliamentary
duties required his presence in town.

At this watering-place, Mrs. Orford and Emily met
in society a person of gentlemanlike appearance, called
'Captain Harcourt'. His manners were prepossessing, his
address unaffected and easy. He was very good-looking,
amusing, and clever, though superficial. He was a great
favourite with the little society, and the young ladies used
to speak of him as 'that charming man'.

Captain Harcourt did not pay Miss Orford the attention she had been accustomed to receive; he seemed
to prefer others who had less pretensions to beauty. He
had never once asked Miss Orford to dance, though he
had been introduced to her, and had met her at several
evening parties. He appeared to hold aloof from Emily,
though he occasionally condescended to converse with
her mother.

Mrs. Orford invited Captain Harcourt to dine at her
house, albeit he had never called upon her. The Captain
accepted the invitation, and after dinner, over the dessert,
culled for Mrs. Orford that bouquet of compliments for
which she had been pining all day long.

At the request of her mother, Emily played and sang; and Captain Harcourt bestowed that languid applause which men of fashion frequently affect. His ears were enchanted by her voice, but he skilfully kept his raptures under control. Emily's sketches, too, were also exhibited for Captain Harcourt's inspection and criticism, and he was pleased to speak of them as 'rather good – not at all bad'.

On taking leave of Mrs. Orford and her daughter, the Captain shook the former's hand very graciously, but gave Emily only two fingers and a very low bow.

On the following day Captain Harcourt met Mrs. Orford and her daughter on the beach. As he approached, Emily blushed, and involuntarily trembled. She knew not why, but she felt ill, and could scarcely refrain from bursting into tears. Captain Harcourt spoke to Emily in a patronising tone of voice, and with the air of a man who feels that his words are valuable. Emily was annoyed; but she could not hate the man. She had now an interest in him. And why? He had piqued her, provoked her.

It is hard to say at what age folly is likely to end in women who have been greatly admired in their youthful days. Mrs. Orford was actually *proud* that Captain Harcourt preferred her conversation to that of her daughter, and had she been a widow, she would have accepted him as a second husband, had he proposed to her.

On taking leave that evening on the beach, Captain Harcourt bestowed upon Emily a warmer shake of the hand than he had given her on the previous night, and smiled upon her. Emily was not prepared for this. It took her by surprise; and the gentle pressure she experienced thrilled through every vein, and made her heart beat violently.

Emily could not sleep that night; she lay awake thinking of Captain Harcourt. She could now feel for poor Charles Everest, for Mr. Hastings, and for Captain Deesing, since she had conceived a love for a man who regarded her with indifference, or who was only civil to her out of mere charity. More than once she summoned all her pride, and tried to laugh at herself for thinking of Captain Harcourt; but that luscious poison of love had entered into her blood, and in vain did she attempt to eject it.

It was Emily's wont to rise early, and walk with her maid by the seashore. While she was dressing on the morning which followed that most eventful evening of her life – Oh! How she longed that she might meet Captain Harcourt! That she might see him, even if it were at a distance! Emily did see him; and when she bowed to him he raised his hat, gave a formal inclination of his head, and, with a smile on his face, passed on.

Captain Harcourt had far more cunning than any of those gentlemen who had aspired to Emily Orford's affections. He knew that the shortest and safest way to a woman's heart and soul was the longest way round, and by the most intricate path. That she was an heiress, and that her father was a man possessed of great parliamentary interest, he had already informed himself.

When Captain Harcourt was convinced that Emily really loved him – after he had observed her keep her eyes upon him for hours together at several parties – he proceeded with immense tact to rivet (if that were necessary) the regard which Emily entertained for him; and one afternoon, when she was walking, alone, on the beach, he came up suddenly and offered his arm.

'I am afraid, Miss Orford, you must often have thought me very uncouth; but, alas! You little know what pain the demeanour I have felt bound to assume has caused me. I am about to leave this place tomorrow, and the chances are we may never meet again, for my regiment is abroad, and I must join it; but before we part, let me assure you that I have not been insensible of your beauty, your talents, your great and varied accomplishments; nor have I been a stranger to the goodness of your heart. I am a proud man, and I have struggled hard to conceal that I loved you, because I would not run the risk of being repulsed by one, the name of whose rejected lovers must already be legion. I would ask you, as a favour, not to think ill of me after I am gone.' And he gently took her hand, and held it in his own.

Emily leaned heavily upon Captain Harcourt's arm, and looked up into his large dark eyes. She could not speak just then, but presently she said, 'Do not go tomorrow. Stay here a little longer.'

'Can it be that your heart beats a response to mine?' he inquired, with well-feigned wonder.

'Yes.' And again she looked into his eyes.

By this time they had rounded the cliff. Not a soul was near them. They were soon pledged to each other, and their pledges witnessed by the wild waves which came dancing to their feet.

Emily was a member of the Catholic Church – so was her mother – though her father was a Protestant. She made this known to Captain Harcourt, who, to her unspeakable joy, did not regard her faith in the light of an impediment to their union. And then the Captain quoted to her those passionate lines of Moore:

On some calm placid shore we'll dwell,
Where 'tis no crime to love too well;
Where thus to worship tenderly
An erring child of light like thee
Would not be sin; or if it be,
Where we might weep our faults away,
Together kneeling night and day;
Thou, for my sake, at Alla's shrine,
And I at *any* God's for thine!

'I have to fear, dearest,' said Captain Harcourt, 'that at present it would be premature to mention our attachment to your excellent mother. For a brief while let it be a secret known only to ourselves. We can meet every morning early, and every afternoon at about this hour; and at our leisure we can settle our plans, dearest Emily. Yes. Since you wish it, I will defer my departure.'

CHAPTER III

DAY AFTER DAY Emily met Captain Harcourt, on the beach; and day after day he tested her regard for him. A woman loses her pride as soon as she ardently loves a man (so far at least as between him and herself), and Emily put up with and endured more of Captain Harcourt's assumed caprice and temper than most people would be inclined to credit. He would sometimes talk of going off immediately by a post-chaise; and the otherwise high-spirited girl would implore him to remain, and not leave her to die of a broken heart. He would at another time recount the girls then at the watering-place who were anxious to elope with him, and hint that he might yet be tempted; and Emily, who was conscious of having done nothing to offend him, would endeavour to assuage his well-acted irritability. Captain Harcourt would at other times insinuate that Emily loved him not for himself, but for his fortune, and his claim to a lofty title on the death of his uncle, the Marquis; and when Emily denied this, he would cry 'Humph!' and curl his moustache with his finger and thumb.

In the innocence of her soul Emily had divulged to the Captain the extent of her affection, and he had determined never to relax that hold which the secret gave him. Her fears that he would leave her, and blight her love, had imparted to Captain Harcourt the bravery of a bully. She often dreaded to meet him on the sands, and yet if he did not keep his engagement she was miserable for the remainder of the day. It was not that Captain Harcourt was a man of *ferocious* disposition; on the contrary, the amenity of his nature was very remarkable.

One morning, shortly after the Captain had created a difference, and Emily's kind words had brought about a reconciliation, Captain Harcourt stopped suddenly, and said, 'Dearest, at the hour of two today, I must leave this place. I must no longer delay. Dallying here has already brought me into disgrace at the Horse Guards. If you will – fly with me. If not, we will say "farewell", forever. A post-chaise will be ready at the hour I mention; and at a quarter past two I will be at the end of the lane, near your mother's house. We can be married in Scotland, dearest. *My* relations will witness the ceremony; and ere long *yours* will be reconciled. You know I love you, Emily – that I worship you. Make up your mind.'

'Dear Reginald,' exclaimed Emily, 'my parents never opposed my will. My mother is kindly disposed towards you; and I am sure you would be a favourite with my father.'

'I am a strange fellow,' said Captain Harcourt. 'From childhood, a creature of impulse; and I shall be the same to the end of the chapter. It was impulse that made me decline running off with the Marchioness of Riggethimbley. It was impulse that made me break off a match with Lady Clorinda Dimsingthorne, after the settlements were concluded. (It is true I did not love her.) It was impulse that made me play for the furniture and fittings-up of a gambling house, and made me lose back £20,000, after I had broken the bank. It is for you, dearest, to decide. Don't do anything in a hurry. There is time, Emily, for consideration, between this and a quarter past two.'

Emily decided, on the spot, that she would elope with Captain Harcourt.

Mrs. Orford and her daughter were engaged to spend that day with some friends, but when twelve o'clock came, Emily said she had a headache, and Mrs. Orford left her house accompanied only by a servant.

Emily was now distracted between her love and her duty. At one moment she decided on abandoning Captain Harcourt, and clinging to those who had, from her infancy, shown her nothing but tenderness and affection. The next moment she would rush into her room, and make preparations for a journey.

The hour of two came. She had but a few minutes to decide. It was impossible to pluck her love from out her bosom – and how could she thus desert her parents?

Five minutes past two! She could not run away. She began to unpack hastily her carpet bags, and replace her dresses in the drawers of her wardrobe; but before the task was done, dear Reginald's eyes seemed to gleam upon her, and she *re*-packed the bags.

Ten minutes past two! She heard the sound of carriage wheels. A carriage had passed the door! She seized her bags – rushed out of the gate, to the end of the lane – met Reginald, who handed her into the post-chaise and kissed her. She fainted on his shoulder as soon as she was seated.

CHAPTER IV

THERE WERE NO electric telegraph despatches in the days when Captain Harcourt carried off Emily Orford – no special trains that could travel at the rate of fifty miles an hour. The fastest conveyance was a post-chaise, and when Mrs. Orford, at four o'clock, was startled by the intelligence that Emily had eloped, she was unable to find out what road even the fugitives had taken. Nevertheless she displayed some show of a pursuit, and made the best of her way to London, where she informed her husband of what had taken place.

Mr. Orford was naturally furious. In vain did Mrs. Orford declare that Captain Harcourt was a most gentlemanlike person, that he was very rich, highly connected, and much courted in society.

Emily was advertised and described in the papers, and a reward of £500 was offered to any person or persons who would prevent the solemnisation of matrimony between herself and the person with whom she had eloped. But these precautions were of no avail. The old blacksmith at Gretna Green had tied the knot before the advertisement appeared at any great distance from London, and Captain Harcourt, in the ecstasy of his joy, presented the blacksmith with a bank note for £50.

Captain Harcourt, that child of impulse, had (to use a vulgar phrase) 'heaps of money', and he squandered it with an open-handedness which surprised even Emily, who had been accustomed to witness a somewhat prodigal liberality on the part of her father; and she playfully rebuked 'Reginald', several times, for his profuseness, but he only kissed her in reply, and remarked, 'What does it signify, Emily, dearest? In what consists the value of wealth but the enjoyment it affords?'

What struck Emily as very strange was this. When Reginald was courting her he was so cross, so irritable, and so overbearing; but now that she was his wife, and completely in his power, he was all submission, and the most good-tempered and obliging creature imaginable. 'So unlike most men,' she reflected, 'who are all honey when they are lovers, but vinegar itself soon after they are married. *Dear* Reginald!' Emily patted the head of the Captain, who pretended to be sleeping, ran her tapering fingers through his luxuriant whiskers, and kissed his forehead.

Reginald shuddered beneath her touch. Emily fancied he was disturbed in his dreams by some horrid vision, and she awakened him. Reginald started up, glared at his wife, and said, 'Remember, dearest Emily, nothing shall ever part us. I love you from the very bottom of my heart. Your father is a member of Parliament, and has enormous influence at the Home Office. Forgive me, darling, if ever I spoke unkindly to you.'

They were now on their way to Matlock from Gretna Green.

At Matlock, Emily, at Captain Harcourt's dictation, wrote several letters to her parents. From her father she never had a reply; but from her mother she received a note in these words: 'Emily – We have brought ourselves to think of you like the rest of our offspring.'

'I say,' said Captain Harcourt, on reading this laconic epistle, 'it won't pay for them to shake us off in that fashion. Our exchequer won't bear that, my girl. We must try a penitent touch. We will give 'em a *quasi pro confesso* go of the pathetic, with a dash of the appeal to a sense of pride, bearing on the merits. Was it for this that I told the old lady, on what I considered the best authority, that George the Fourth turned out the Ministry, because the Secretary of State for Foreign Affairs would not consent to having her husband made a baronet, so much was his Majesty struck with her personal beauty, when she appeared at the drawing room? Oh, hang it, Emmy, this will never do!'

Emily could not understand either the tone or the substance of Reginald's observations; but then, Reginald was often so incoherently funny that she did not attempt to unravel his sentences. She therefore contented herself with smiling, and saying, 'Never mind, dearest Reginald; when you come in for your title, on your uncle's death, my mother, who is very proud and vain – bless her dear heart! – will be only too glad to acknowledge and receive us; and, if it be possible, we shall be happier then than we are now, my own dear Reginald.'

'What sort of a man is your father, really?' inquired Captain Harcourt. 'Is he a man of warm feelings, generously disposed?'

Emily described her father truly, as 'the kindest and most liberal-minded man in the world, and very intellectual withal, but rather obstinate and determined.'

'That's all right,' said Captain Harcourt. 'Then I know how to deal with him.' And the Captain, who was rather overcome by constant refreshment taken during that day, sat down, and, in a handwriting resembling copperplate, wrote the following. (The verses he italicised.)

EDMUND ORFORD, Esq., M.P., &C., &C., &C.,

SIR – Pardon me; but I desire to make an explanation: I am sure you will forgive me.

> The faults of love by love are justified,
> With unresisted might the monarch reigns,
> He levels mountains and he raises plains,
> And, not regarding difference of degree,
> Abased your daughter and exalted me.

Yours obediently,

REGINALD HARCOURT.

It is needless, perhaps, to say that Mr. Orford never took the slightest notice of this communication. It confirmed his previously conceived opinion that 'Captain Harcourt' was some low blackguard – an impostor and a swindler.

CHAPTER V

CAPTAIN AND MRS. Harcourt went to Brighton, and there rented a house in a very quiet neighbourhood. For several months Emily was as happy as a woman constantly in the society of a man whom she loves can make herself. She now and then regretted that she had left her home so abruptly, but a kind word from her husband speedily put her sorrow to flight.

The Captain told Emily that it was his intention to 'sell out', since he feared taking her to such a bad climate as that of the West Indies, where his regiment was quartered; and he wrote several letters to the Horse Guards on the subject of retiring from the service, and gave Emily to understand that he was going out to post them; but instead of doing this, he tore them up in a public house, and converted them into pipe-lights; for wedlock had in no way diminished the Captain's taste for tobacco and gin-and-water.

Over his pipe and his glass, in the back parlour of a tavern, Captain Harcourt would sit gloomily. He appeared to have something on his mind, and to feel relieved by these stolen visits to the various public houses. The aroma consequent on smoking and drinking he dispelled by chewing lemon peel previous to rejoining his wife; and from this the reader will conclude that the Captain was not altogether destitute of consideration for Emily's feelings.

One morning at breakfast, Captain Harcourt suddenly threw down the newspaper which he was reading, became deadly pale and much agitated.

Emily was alarmed, and wished to send for a doctor. 'No, dearest,' the Captain said. 'It is only a passing spasm. I shall be better presently.'

During the whole of that day, however, the Captain seemed very unwell. He complained of a bad headache, and a pain in the side, expressed a fear that the air of Brighton did not agree with him, and proposed seeking a change by going that night to Portsmouth. Emily, who never opposed Reginald's wishes, declared herself quite ready. A post-chaise was instantly ordered, their trunks speedily packed, and, at ten o'clock, Captain and Mrs. Harcourt were away from Brighton.

'It was all the air,' said the Captain, when they had travelled about five miles. 'I knew it was. I feel better already. My spirits are quite buoyant. I feel now up to all sorts of fun.' And to prove this, the Captain took off Emily's bonnet, put it upon his own head, tied her boa closely round his neck, and a scarf over his mouth, put on his wife's spare cloak, thrust his hands into a muff, and said, 'Emmy dear, should I not make a capital woman? Put my hair in paper, dearest, three curls on each side. Is it long enough, darling?'

'Oh, quite long enough, Reginald dear,' said Emily; and by the moon's light she gratified her husband's funny humour, and tightly twisted up his hair, according to his directions, 'three curls on each side'.

Captain Harcourt did make an excellent woman, for a very inquisitive and impertinent man, who had been following the post-chaise on horseback, opened the door, and peered in, when they stayed to pay the first toll, and, after satisfying his curiosity, said, 'Two ladies: all right. Beg your pardon.'

The Captain's funny humour, this whim of his, lasted all night. He went to sleep (?) in the curl papers and Emily's bonnet, and did not divest himself of the female attire till daylight next morning.

'What a funny creature you are, Reginald,' said Emily, while she was combing out the Captain's curls.

'Always was,' he replied. 'Child of impulse, Emmy.'

~

Having arrived in safety at Portsmouth, Captain and Mrs. Harcourt took a small cottage, and enjoyed the sweets of solitude for several weeks. But one night, alas! A coarse man, in top-boots and corduroy breeches, and a blue double-breasted coat, with brass buttons upon it, without being announced, broke in upon them, and said, in the most familiar manner, to the Captain, 'Hulloa, nay pippin! Oh! Charley!'

Captain Harcourt was naturally very indignant, and asked the intruder what he meant. The intruder in reply put out his tongue at the Captain, squinted hideously, and drew from his pocket a piece of parchment.

Captain Harcourt protested that it was all a mistake; and Emily's anger now being aroused, she desired the intruder to leave the house.

'I will do that immediately, mam,' said the intruder. 'But you'll excuse me for saying that this gentleman, the Captain – Captain Harcourt – mam – the Captain, mam

– the Captain must go along with me. Particular business demands it, mam.'

'Emily, dearest,' said Captain Harcourt, in a whisper, 'I am not the first person in the world that has been subjected to inconvenience by a false identity. It once happened to the great Duke of Marlborough – ay, royalty itself has not escaped. Compose yourself, dearest. By going at once it will be the sooner over. The law shall be altered. I will soon be back. Now, don't cry, that's a darling.'

CHAPTER VI

EMILY FANCIED THAT her husband had been arrested for the debt of some other person. She had no idea of the truth – that he had been apprehended on a *criminal* charge. He had been absent ten days and had never written to her. She did not reproach him, because she imagined his time was wholly engaged in clearing up this unfortunate mistake. Her fears were for poor Reginald's health. What pained her most was that she could not write to him, for she did not know his address; and this put her to some inconvenience, insomuch as he had only left her a few pounds, which were now almost exhausted. All their ready money, some two or three hundred pounds, Reginald had thoughtlessly carried away with him.

Captain Harcourt, when at Portsmouth, used to receive regularly the *Examiner* newspaper, and it was from this journal Emily learnt that, under the name of Charles Roberts, her husband had been arraigned and tried at the Central Criminal Court for having on a certain day forged a certain deed, by which the Bank of England had been defrauded by the said Charles Roberts of a certain sum of money, to wit, the sum of £7,850. And alas! She further learnt that he had been found guilty, and sentenced to be transported to New South Wales for the term of his natural life!

Charles Roberts, *alias* Reginald Harcourt, had retained as his counsel Mr. Hastings, the 'rising barrister', who had formerly been a suitor for Emily's hand, and most ably did his counsel perform his painful but bounden duty. Mr. Hastings's speech – which Emily entirely agreed with, fancying that it came from the counsel's heart – was ingenious and eloquent in the extreme; but the evidence was much too clear, and the proof of Roberts's identity (the great point in dispute) much too strong to be shaken by an artful cross-examination, or explained away by rhetorical flourishes.

Emily could not believe that her husband was guilty of the offence, and, having pawned her watch and dressing case, at the suggestion of one of her servants, she hasted to town. She did not dare to visit her father; she knew his stern, unbending disposition too well to warrant her harbouring a thought or cherishing a hope that he would ever forgive her or raise his voice on behalf of her unfortunate husband. And, harder still, she felt that her mother's implacability would not be one whit inferior to that of Mr. Orford himself. She had many friends in London, yet she knew not which of them to consult in a matter so difficult and so peculiarly delicate. At length it occurred to her that she could not do better than select the gentleman who had expressed at the trial such positive opinions respecting Reginald's innocence.

Emily had listened with a cold ear to the outpourings of his warm heart, and she had refused his hand, if not with disdain, with something which very much resembled it: still, she determined to plead for her husband at the feet of her rejected lover. It was easy to procure his address. She found it in the *Court Guide*. 'George Hastings, King's Bench Walk, Temple.'

With trembling hand Emily touched the knocker of the door, over which this name was painted in large black letters. The door was opened by a clerk, who informed Emily that Mr. Hastings was at present engaged at a consultation, but if she pleased to wait until it was over she could see him. Emily took a chair in the clerk's room; she could hear Mr. Hastings's voice in the next apartment, not as she had been wont to hear it, soft-toned and gentle, but loud, and rather imperious and overbearing.

The consultation over, Emily heard the clerk say to Mr. Hastings, 'Please, sir, there's a lady wishes to see you.'

'A what?' said Mr. Hastings, abruptly.

'A lady, please, sir,' replied the clerk, timidly.

'What does she want?' inquired Mr. Hastings.

'To see you, sir!'

'Why, you fool, you've told me that already. What is her *business*?'

'That I don't know, sir. I tried to find out. But I couldn't glean it, sir.'

'Has she come alone?'

'Yes, sir.'

'Well, admit her.'

'If you please, ma'am, will you walk this way?' said the clerk to Emily.

Who shall describe the emotions of the man when his eyes fell upon the woman whom he still devotedly loved; when he beheld her, pale and agitated, sink into a chair and give vent to a violent flood of tears; when he heard her, far more eloquent than he had been at the trial, protesting the innocence of the most artful and worthless villain whom it had ever been his, Mr. Hastings's, lot to defend? Mr. Hastings could not explain to Emily that his opinions, which she quoted to him, were intended only for the jury, and that no one more entirely concurred in the justice of the verdict than he, Mr. Hastings, did. In pity for her sufferings he made no attempt to dispel the delusion under which she was labouring. Emily begged of him to use his influence and cause the sentence to be reversed, and she piteously extracted from him a promise that he would befriend her in her serious difficulties. And she asked him where 'poor Reginald' was to be found. Mr. Hastings had not the courage to tell her this. 'Reginald' was in the hulks, dressed in the attire of a convict, and shorn of his moustache and long, silky dark brown hair.

Emily called the next day at the chambers in King's Bench Walk, and was informed by the clerk that Mr. Hastings had been obliged to leave town suddenly, and would not return for several weeks!

Charles Everest was now a clerk in the Home Office. Mr. Hastings, in reply to a question put by Emily, had stated that the Home Secretary was the only person who had the power of saving her husband. Emily sought an interview with Charles Everest, and Charles Everest spoke to the Home Secretary. The Home Secretary could not, of course, listen to his intercession.

On her way from the Home Office to her lodging, Emily met, near the Horse Guards, a captain in the navy – Captain Bruce – an old and intimate friend of the Orford family. Emily unbosomed her sorrows to Captain Bruce, but he was unable to offer her any assistance or advice, except that which she could not follow.

CHAPTER VII

CAPTAIN BRUCE TOOK Emily to his home in the country, where himself, his wife, and his daughters endeavoured to make her troubles less difficult to bear. Here Emily had a serious illness, and during its continuance her reason frequently deserted her. When she recovered, she expressed a wish to follow her convict husband, in whose innocence she still firmly believed, to New South Wales, and share his lot, whatever it might be. The folly, the madness of this proposal were forcibly pointed out by Captain and Mrs. Bruce, and by other friends. But Emily still remained steadfast in her resolve.

Captain Bruce, who was not rich, had a large family to support. To convey Emily to Australia was more than his means could compass. He therefore resorted to a subscription among his most intimate friends, and succeeded in raising the sum of £125.

Captain Bruce saw Emily on board the ship which was to carry her to New South Wales, and was shocked to think that such a gentle, graceful being, who had been brought up from her infancy with so much tenderness and care, should be thus thrown amongst the mass of people then standing on the vessel's deck. Some hundreds of trunks and carpet bags were strewed about in all directions. Scores of voices were raised in contention with the mates and other persons in authority on board. Men, women, and children, in rags, were wandering about, inquiring where they were to be stowed. Some looked as though they had seen better days, and regretted leaving their native land now that they were about to sail; others, as though their days and nights had been spent in debauchery, and that any change that might come must be for the better. Emily appeared to take little heed of the miserable creatures around her. She was indifferent about her own comfort, and dead to everything except the desire of seeing and again living with her husband.

~

Emily was under the impression that she would have a cabin to herself, but of this idea her mind was speedily disabused. She had only 'a berth' in an apartment between decks, in common with nine other females, steerage passengers. She was rather disappointed at this; but her joy at the idea of being at last actually on the way to Sydney, to join dear Reginald, would not suffer the inconvenience to which she was subjected to give her any serious annoyance.

Four of Emily's cabin companions were women of respectable appearance and steady mien; three were persons of doubtful character and frivolous manners, while the remaining two, from the style of their conversation, and the grossness of their discourse, must have led the most dissolute and abandoned of lives. Emily often trembled and shuddered at their horrid stories, which she could not help hearing, for these two women invariably talked in a loud tone, as though they were rather proud of their opinions, and thought it a pity that any of them should be lost by the limited community of which they formed a part.

One evening, near the equator, Emily observed that the playful banter in which these eloquent damsels were indulging was about to lead to a violent encounter, and she ventured, in the kindest and gentlest manner possible, to address them, in the hope not of adjusting their differences – that would have been impossible, for they invariably quarrelled about *nothing* – but of averting a disgraceful outbreak. The consequence of Emily's interference was that she brought upon herself the combined forces of these capricious women, who, disturbed in the amusement which quarrelling seemed to afford them, first asked her – or rather said they should 'like to know' who *she* was – what she meant, what business she had to put *her* finger into other people's pies; and before Emily had time to reply – even had she been able to do so – they called her a variety of names, of which – fortunately for her own peace of mind – she had not the most remote idea of the meaning. Emily made no complaint of this treatment, but the captain of the vessel, happening to be informed of it, immediately made arrangements which secured for her both privacy and comparative comfort during the remainder of the voyage.

When the land was sighted Emily became agitated and nervous. All sorts of horrible fancies filled her distracted mind. Amongst other things, she feared her husband might have sunk under the weight of his misfortunes, and died in a distant land without any friend near him to close his eyes, and administer comfort to his departing spirit.

Emily had of late frequently conversed with Captain Dent, the commander of the *Lady Jane Grey*, and had received many little attentions and kindnesses at his hands. Being herself perfectly ignorant of everything relating to the colony, and as Captain Dent had been frequently to the port of Sydney, she made bold to question him one afternoon, when a good opportunity presented itself, respecting a few matters on which she needed some definite information.

Emily prefaced her questions with a brief sketch of her history, and failed not to dwell particularly upon the innocence of her husband, whom she declared had been transported entirely by mistake. This part of her narrative Captain Dent did not implicitly believe; but he could see that Emily was quite sincere in her protestations.

Captain Dent was a kind-hearted, fatherly old gentleman, and he pitied Emily, felt for her as though she had been a child of his own. He promised her that she should be comfortably housed on her arrival in Sydney, and pledged himself to spare no pains, as soon as he could afford time, in ascertaining in what part of the colony her husband might be located. Emily fancied she might ascertain this by inquiring at the post office, but Captain Dent very delicately gave her to understand that persons in her husband's unfortunate predicament had rarely any settled address, and that it was sometimes rather difficult to find them, although everybody knew they were somewhere in the colony.

'For instance,' said Captain Dent, 'he may be in Sydney, or he may be in Paramatta, or in Windsor, or at Bathurst, or on some farm in the distant interior.'

'On some farm!' said Emily. 'No, I don't think dear Reginald would turn farmer, though I should like him to do so, I confess; for we could then live on some secluded spot, where we might never see a soul from one year's end to another.'

CHAPTER VIII

THE EMIGRANT SHIP dropped her anchor in the harbour of Port Jackson. Had Emily's mind been at ease, how busy would she have been, sketching the magnificent scenery that now met her view.

Numbers of persons came on board, and most of the emigrants were engaged at once; those who were not so fortunate landed to search for employ. Amongst the latter were the two young women who had behaved so badly to Emily, and conducted themselves so boisterously on the voyage. Captain Dent took Emily to the house of a very respectable widow, who used to let furnished apartments. It was at her house, when he lived on shore, that Captain Dent had, for years past, taken up his abode. He advised Emily, as they walked up George Street, not to mention to the widow anything concerning her husband, and remain as quiet as possible.

'Why?' inquired Emily.

'You had better not say anything about your husband,' repeated Captain Dent. He longed to tell her, but had not the heart to wound her feelings, that persons who, like the widow, had gone out 'free' to Australia would object to receive into their houses, under any circumstances, the wife of a person under sentence of transportation. 'Remain quiet,' urged the old Captain, 'until I see you again. It may be tomorrow evening.'

When Captain Dent had left her, and returned to the ship, Emily felt unable to keep her promise. She could not rest, tired as she was with the exertion of packing up her trunks and preparing to land. Reginald, she thought, might be within a short distance of her – perhaps in the same street, or even next door – who could tell? Dear Reginald! Oh, what happiness to meet him that night! To put his long dark hair off his beautiful white forehead, and kiss the poor innocent dear who was the victim of a base conspiracy! How could she exist in such painful suspense? So she sent for the landlady, Mrs. White.

'Could you oblige me', said Emily, 'with the sight of a directory? I should be very much obliged to you if you would, Mrs. White. I wish to find out the address of a gentleman whom I know.'

'A directory, mum?' said Mrs. White. 'There's no directory published in the colony; but we have almanacs. There's no need of directories, mum; everybody knows where everybody else lives. If you'll tell me the name of any gentleman, I have no doubt I shall be able to give you his address.'

'Oh! Could you?' cried Emily, overcome by her anxiety, and seizing Mrs. White by the hand. 'His name is Harcourt – Reginald Harcourt.'

'Captain Harcourt, mum?' said Mrs. White.

'Yes, Captain Harcourt!' said Emily. 'Do tell me, where is he to be found?'

'Captain Harcourt, mum, whom I know very well, is not in Sydney just now. When in Sydney, he lives in the barracks in his quarters; but he married only a few days ago, and he has gone into the country with his bride!'

'Married!' cried Emily. 'Married! Impossible! How could he marry, when I am his wife?'

'It must be someone else, mum, whom you mean,' said Mrs. White. 'Captain Harcourt has been very wild, and often does very funny things, and enjoys a joke, like most of the officers; but I don't think he would commit bigamy. That's rather too much of a good thing.'

'Do you know any other Captain Harcourt?' asked Emily, in an agony of impatience.

'No, mum,' said Mrs. White. 'The only Captain Harcourt in the colony, I believe, is *the* Captain Harcourt I have spoken of.'

'Describe him – *do* describe him,' said Emily; for she really began to have some misgivings that Reginald had forgotten her and himself. 'Tell me, Mrs. White, is he tall? Handsome? Clever?'

'No, mum; he is short, stout, and plain,' replied Mrs. White. 'As to "cleverness", I can't say, of that I am no judge; but he is a great favourite with the ladies.'

Though Emily's mind was at once relieved of the horrible idea that 'dear Reginald' might possibly have married some other lady to keep his house, and look after his comforts, still her anxiety to be informed of his whereabouts was increased rather than diminished.

'And you know of no other Captain Harcourt or *Mr.* Harcourt?' she again asked Mrs. White.

'No, mum; I am quite sure there is no other person of the name in the colony,' said Mrs. White.

'See here,' said Emily, wildly. 'I will tell you all, Mrs. White; and then you may be able to assist me. Pray sit down. Excuse my troubling you in this way; but if you only knew' – here she burst into tears – 'what I have suffered, and what I now suffer, I am sure you would pity me. Pray sit down, Mrs. White.'

Mrs. White took a chair. Emily sat opposite to her, and divulged the sad tale. She was several times interrupted by convulsive sobbing, and Mrs. White was a good deal affected by the narrative. Mrs. White acknowledged that she knew nothing of Roberts (Emily was obliged to say that his accusers persisted in calling him Roberts); but if Emily could give her the name of the ship which brought him to the colony, and the date of his sailing from England, she said she could easily ascertain by inquiring at the office in Hyde Park. Emily said the name of the vessel was the *Medora*, and that it was exactly a year since her husband had left home.

'The *Medora*!' said Mrs. White. 'I have an assigned servant who came out in that ship, and perhaps he may know something about him. They generally do know all about their shipmates – to whom they are assigned, or whether they are reserved for government's own employ, in the offices, or dockyards, or barracks.'

'But a good deal depends on what he was at home,' Mrs. White added. 'If he knows any trade——'

'Trade!' exclaimed Emily, interrupting her. 'Trade! My husband was a gentleman – an officer.'

'Oh! Indeed!' said Mrs. White. 'I beg your pardon. Yes, you mentioned that his name was Harcourt, and came out here by mistake for a person called Roberts. In former days gentlemen were called 'specials', and were sent to a place called Wellington Valley, but there is no distinction made now; all are treated alike, gentle and simple. All are assigned to take their chance.'

'How do you mean assigned?' inquired Emily.

'Why, when one wants servants, male or female,' said Mrs. White, 'one applies for them, and government are only too glad to get them off their hands. They do all your work, and you clothe them and feed them. This young man who was assigned to me out of the *Medora* was very well-to-do in Dublin, and his father, who is a clergyman, keeps his carriage; but the young man was transported for some offence or other, and was assigned to me.'

'Poor young man!' said Emily. 'And perhaps he was just as innocent as my husband was.'

'I have no doubt of that,' returned Mrs. White, meaning what she said, but not in the sense in which Emily received the remark.

'And do you think he knows what has become of my Reginald?' inquired Emily.

'Most likely,' said Mrs. White. 'He will be home presently, and I will ask him.'

'And how do you employ the young man?' said Emily.

'He chops the wood, cleans the boots and shoes, and the knives, runs errands, answers the door, and makes himself generally useful; and if he doesn't, I stop his tea and sugar, and put him on gov'ment allowance – ten pound of flour and seven pound of beef a week, and make him cook it himself,' said Mrs. White.

'Poor thing!' cried Emily, shuddering from head to foot, lest she should hear that 'Reginald' was in similar circumstances.

A woman came in, and delivered some message to her mistress. When she had left the room, Emily inquired, 'Is that woman a convict?'

'Yes,' said Mrs. White. 'But never use the word "convict" unless you are in a passion, and wish to wound their feelings. "Convict" is a word they cannot bear. Always speak of them as "assigned servants", or "prisoners of the Crown"; these are milder terms, you know.'

Mrs. White heard the manservant's voice in the kitchen, and said to Emily, 'If you will excuse me for a few minutes I will see if Nelson has returned.'

'Nelson,' said Mrs. White, 'was there a man named Roberts, *alias* Harcourt, on board the *Medora*?'

(Nelson, according to his own account, was the eldest son of a rector in Ireland, who belonged to the elder branch of the family rendered so illustrious by our greatest naval hero. This statement, however, was open to very grave question, for not only had Nelson's education been confined to the merest rudiments, and not only was his countenance of a cast which was prodigiously plebeian, but he had been transported for an offence which, to say the least of it, was not by any means such as a gentleman 'born and bred' would ever think of committing. It was for picking an old woman's pocket at a fair of a silk handkerchief, a bunch of keys, and a brass thimble. But, insomuch as most young men in similar circumstances, and especially those from Ireland, were prone to indulge in making out that they were 'very well connected at home', some excuse may be made for Nelson's desire to exalt himself at the expense of his veracity. Not that it made much difference with Mrs. White.)

'Yes, mum,' said Nelson, in reply to Mrs. White's question. 'Roberts, *alias* Harcourt. He was a flash fellow, who was lagged for forgery: he used to boast of having great parliamentary influence, which was to procure him a free pardon and apartments in Government House on landing.

He was employed in the Auditor-General's office, being a clever hand with his pen; but he soon misconducted himself, and was put into barracks. After that he was drawn by Mr. Dawson, of Campbell Town, and put to pig feeding; but he has run away, it seems, and is advertised in today's *Gazette*, with a reward of £10 offered for his apprehension.'

'Run over the way, and see if you can borrow the paper,' said Mrs. White. 'Don't be long.'

Nelson went, and in a few minutes returned with the paper. There could be no mistake about the person. The advertisement ran as follows:

> Whereas, my assigned servant, Charles Roberts, *alias* Harcourt, per ship *Medora*, under sentence of transportation for life, absconded from my employ, on the night of the 13th instant, this is to give notice that a reward of £10 sterling will be paid to any person or persons who will give such information as will lead to his apprehension. Description: name, Charles Roberts, *alias* Harcourt; ship, *Medora*; sentence, life; height, 5 feet 11¾; age, 33; complexion, fair; eyes, hazel; hair, dark brown; whiskers, black; figure, slight; trade or calling, clerk; marks, small scar on upper lip, scar on the back of left hand, mole on the left breast.
>
> N.B.—The absentee has white and very regular teeth, plausible manners and graceful bearing; at the time he ran away he was dressed in a striped shirt, duck trousers, white smock frock, high-low shoes, Scotch cap, and a blue bird's-eye pocket-handkerchief tied round his neck. He is

supposed to have gone to Sydney, with a view of making his escape from the colony.

James Dawson, Campbell Town.

'What a villain!' exclaimed Mrs. White, putting down the paper. 'I should not be surprised to hear he has turned bushranger.'

'No chance of that, mum,' said Nelson. 'He was one of those fellows who would talk the hind leg off a dog, but would not have the courage to face a small boy or a big musquito. Laziness has made him run away; and when he sees the advertisement in the paper he will get frightened, and give himself up, mum.'

Mrs. White was afraid to give Emily these tidings of her husband, lest they should cause her a fit of illness and detain her in the house for some days. She could not help pitying Emily, but felt that it would be extremely prejudicial to her own interests to permit a person whom she knew to be the wife of a convict, and that convict a runaway – perhaps a bushranger – to stay under her roof, even for a short time, as a lodger. Mrs. White, therefore, returned to Emily, and regretted that her servant Nelson could give no information of Roberts's locality. She then recommended Emily to take some repose, and be prepared to get up very early in the morning and accompany her (Mrs. White) to the house of a person who was a clerk in a government office, and who would be sure to know where her husband was to be found.

'Could we not go tonight, if you are not too much fatigued?' inquired Emily.

'Impossible!' said Mrs. White. 'The person whom I mean lives a long way off. Go to rest now, and you will rise quite refreshed, and able to set out on your journey in the morning.'

Emily went to bed, but could not sleep. If she closed her eyes for a moment, the most frightful visions presented themselves. She saw her husband dancing before her in chains, or standing on a platform which they told her was a gallows; or, tied to a cart's tail, he was being flogged, and his blood streaming on the road; or, flying from his pursuers, he was shot, wounded in several parts of the body, and dragged to prison by the hair of his head. Thus disturbed, she remained awake the whole night, till the daylight, for which she so anxiously watched, came streaming through the chinks in the shutters. Emily sprang up, and hurriedly attired herself; but just as she was putting on her bonnet, the woman servant knocked at her door.

'Oh, pray come in!' cried out Emily. 'I am quite ready. Come in, Mrs. White.'

The servant entered, and said, 'Please, mum, it's me. I am sorry to say missis was taken very dangerously ill in the night, mum. We had to fetch the doctor, and thought she would have died, mum. We were going to wake *you*, mum, at one time, to come down and see missis; but we did not like to disturb you, mum, as we thought you were tired.'

'I wish you had called me – I was awake,' said Emily. 'But I hope she is better now?'

'Oh yes, mum, thank you, missis *is* a little better,' replied the woman. 'But the doctor says, mum, that she must be moved immediately off the ground floor where she now is; and there is no other room but this, mum.'

'Dear me, how unfortunate!' exclaimed Emily, abstractedly, gazing out of the window. 'Oh, of course,' added she, recollecting herself, 'I will vacate the room at once; put me anywhere you please.'

'But unfortunately, mum, we have nowhere to put you,' said the woman. 'The room that missis is now in must be given up to the nurse, who has been sent for. She has a little girl that always comes with her, mum, and she cannot do without a room to herself.'

'Do you know of any other respectable lodgings?' inquired Emily.

'No, mum, I do not,' said the servant (for her mistress had told her exactly what to say). 'But it strikes me, mum, that the best thing you could do would be to go on board the ship, where you could have a nice cabin, now that the passengers are all out of her, and there stay, mum, till missis is better, or till you can get a house. As missis is now asleep, mum, I can go with you to the wharf, and hire a waterman's boat for you, which will take you on board, and Nelson will wheel your boxes on the barrow, mum.'

Emily instantly adopted the suggestion, and thanked the woman for her kind offer. 'At all events,' the unhappy lady reasoned, 'I shall see Captain Dent the sooner, and he may have heard something by this time about my poor Reginald.'

CHAPTER IX

WHAT WAS CAPTAIN Dent's astonishment on seeing Emily and her boxes alongside the *Lady Jane Grey*. The vessel was lying out in the stream, and no companion ladder was yet rigged. The chair was lowered, and Emily once more stood upon the deck, where all was in the same state of confusion that she beheld on embarking at Gravesend. When she told the Captain what had passed on the previous night, he could easily comprehend Mrs. White's sudden and serious illness. He was vexed that Emily had been so imprudent as to tell Mrs. White so much of her history, especially as she had been warned not to do so; but, poor creature, he thought she had enough agony of mind to bear already, without having her sufferings aggravated by any useless reproaches, and he therefore withheld them.

Emily's eyelids were red and swollen with weeping, her cheeks very pale, and her limbs so feeble she could scarcely stand.

Captain Dent ordered Emily's boxes to be placed in one of the stern cabins, and caused to be removed from his own a couch, a table, and an easychair. The chief mate contributed a looking glass and a toilet-table; and the second mate gave her some red damask curtains to keep out the glare of noonday, and obstruct the view of persons approaching or leaving the ship.

'You must not tease me now,' said the Captain to Emily in a gentle tone of voice, and with a cheering smile on his lips. 'You must have some breakfast in your cabin, and then you must take a composing draught, and lie down. You had no sleep last night. At two o'clock we will dine, and then I will manage to go onshore with you, and devote myself to your service.'

Emily, who was fairly exhausted with fatigue, felt like a child in the hands of the Captain, and promised to obey all his commands. She took the draught and slept soundly, through all the noise and bustle on board the ship.

~

Refreshed in mind and body, Emily awoke about one o'clock, and prepared for dinner. The dress she wore on this occasion was a very becoming one – a plain black silk, without any kind of ornament except a small topaz brooch, 'Reginald's' first present to her. The people on board had never seen her look so well or so cheerful. She was still, perhaps, under the influence of the opiate – that is to say, the happy feeling which the drug often produces had not entirely departed.

Captain Dent and Emily landed at a place called Dawes's Battery, at about a quarter past three in the afternoon. Thence they proceeded, on foot, through the government domain, towards that part of the town where they were most likely to find a small furnished cottage to be let on moderate terms. On the way Captain Dent espied, at a distance, a gang of convicts heavily ironed, and guarded by some half-dozen soldiers, mending the roads. He immediately led his charge in another direction, to avoid them, for he feared it was just possible that 'Reginald' might be one of that gang, and that Emily might recognise him, when an unpleasant scene would to a certainty ensue. Before Emily could be prevailed upon to look for a cottage, she wished the Captain to take her to the office which Mrs. White had mentioned – the office where she would learn her husband's address. The Captain objected to this, insomuch as he thought it would be more satisfactory for him to go alone to the office. Emily, however, was so earnest, so eloquent in her entreaties, indeed she so piteously implored him, that he was compelled to yield to her request. Accordingly, he shaped his course for the office of the Superintendent of Police, where the name, description, and character of every person who had been transported to Sydney, from the foundation of the colony up to that date, were duly registered. They arrived at and entered the office, Emily leaning on Captain Dent's arm. He wished to leave her below while he went upstairs, but she clung to him, and heard all that passed between himself and one of the clerks, whom he addressed across a counter, whereon were spread a number of books, like ledgers of colossal proportions.

'Could you give me any information,' said Captain Dent, 'respecting a person named Harcourt, or Roberts, who came out last year in the ship *Medora*?'

'No, sir,' said the clerk, smiling. 'I wish I could.'

'A tall gentleman, sir, with dark eyes,' said Emily, anxious to assist the clerk's memory.

'Oh, thank you, mum; I know the gentleman's description perfectly,' said the clerk, 'though I have not had the pleasure of seeing him.'

'I thought you knew where every person who came to the colony in an unfortunate position was to be found?' said Captain Dent.

'We know where they *ought* to be found,' replied the clerk, 'but they don't always stop there.'

At this moment a messenger brought into the office, and laid upon the counter, a huge load of placards, printed in monster type. The clerk withdrew one of these placards from a bundle labelled 'Roberts, *alias* Harcourt', and handed it to Captain Dent. This placard contained the substance of the advertisement in the *Gazette*, and it was about to be posted on the walls of every court, police office, prison, and marketplace in every town in the colony, and upon many of the prominent trees on the sides of the highroads.

Emily's eyes hastily scanned the placard; but she had not read the whole of it, when she clasped her hands, uttered a piercing shriek, and fell senseless on the floor!

~

In those days there were no vehicles for hire in the colony, and Captain Dent had to walk with, or rather to carry, his unfortunate charge through the streets. When they were on their way from the shore to the ship, Emily, having recovered from her swoon, stared wildly at the Captain, and then attempted to leap overboard; but the old man kept his arm tightly around her waist, and in spite of her struggles detained her in his grasp. The shock had been too much for her, and she was now insane. It was with the greatest difficulty that she was removed from the boat, and secured in the stern cabin.

In a few days Emily's insanity became less violent in character, and gradually it assumed that melancholy from which it is so difficult to arouse the patient.

The *Lady Jane Grey* had suffered some injury on the voyage out, and it was necessary to heave her down to repair it. This rendered it impossible for Emily to remain any longer on board, and Captain Dent, therefore, hired for her a small furnished cottage at the end of a street called Castlereagh Street.

~

The *Lady Jane Grey* had been repaired, filled with oil, wool, &c., and Captain Dent was now ready to sail, via Cape Horn. Again the old man implored Emily to return with him to England. Her obstinacy, such he termed it, had severely tried his patience, and one evening he spoke of the convict Roberts as an incorrigible blackguard, who had married her under false pretences and a false name, and who, therefore, had no claim upon her affections. But Emily thought differently.

'Knowing as I do,' said she, 'that what you have just expressed, Captain Dent, was dictated by the kindest feelings, and remembering, as I do, how much gratitude I owe you, I cannot be angry; but I implore you not to speak again unfavourably of a man whom I have loved, whom I still love, and whom I shall continue to love, believing him to be innocent. So long as he may remain in this uncouth and cruel land, here also will I remain; and whatever may be his sufferings, he shall have that consolation which a wife's sympathy ought ever to afford. I would rather work beside him upon the roads, with fetters on my feet, share with him the coarsest food, and a bed of straw, than return to the home of my father or my friends, and partake of all the comforts, luxuries, and gaiety that once fell to my lot.'

With tears in his eyes the old ship captain raised Emily's thin hand to his lips, and, kissing it affectionately, bade her 'farewell'.

CHAPTER X

NELSON, MRS. WHITE'S assigned servant, was out one evening on an errand. Walking down 'Brick-field Hill', he met Roberts, who was disguised in person as well as in dress.

'Hulloa! Is that you?' said Nelson.

Roberts started, and, giving Nelson a look which was meant to say, 'You have made a mistake,' he moved on. Nelson followed him, and, walking by his side, said, 'It's of no use your attempting to deceive me. I know you; but I am not going to split. Just come and treat me, and I will tell you something which you'll be glad to hear, perhaps.'

After looking round to see that there was no one near, Roberts, feeling that he was in Nelson's power, replied, 'Sam, I'll make it all right with you.'

The two convicts proceeded to a public house, called the 'Wheat Sheaf', where Roberts ordered half a pint of rum, and pipes and tobacco for two. When they had seated themselves in the corner of the tap, and had drunk 'luck' to each other, Roberts commenced the dialogue.

'What's this you have to tell me?' he inquired.

'Perhaps you know,' said Nelson.

'Perhaps I do,' said Roberts, 'but what is it?'

'It won't do beating about the bush,' said Nelson, blowing

a dense cloud of smoke, and watching the festoons vanish as they neared the ceiling.

'No,' said Roberts, knocking the ashes out of his pipe upon the table, 'no, don't beat about the bush, Sam.'

'I say, Charley,' said Nelson, resting his elbows on the table, and placing his chin between the palms of his hands, 'where's your wife?'

Roberts replied, 'I forget now where her last letter was dated from.'

'Where is she, I say?' returned Nelson.

'At home in England with her friends,' said Roberts, 'unless she has taken the office of Maid of Honour to the Queen, as perhaps she will do, just to exert her influence, and procure my free pardon.'

'That's all you know about it,' said Nelson. 'I've seen your wife, talked to her, received coin from her hand. Believe me, or believe me not, but it's true, so——'

'None of your nonsense,' said Roberts.

'There you go, again!' cried Nelson.

'Don't talk so loud,' said Roberts. 'I am not deaf.'

'Then hear this,' said Nelson, in a whisper. 'She is in Sydney; and if you can make it worth my while, and will meet me at the marketplace at ten o'clock tonight, you shall see her at a quarter to eleven.'

'You are chaffing me,' said Roberts. 'You want time to give the office, and have me taken. You think it would make you good for a ticket of leave. I see your dodge, Sam.'

'No, Charley, believe me, on my honour, you are mistaken,' said Nelson. 'I know I'm a convicted villain, but I have still a lingering regard for friendship, and all that sort of thing; and what I have spoken is the truth. Your wife is in Sydney. If you doubt it, I'll describe her.'

'Do,' said Roberts, eagerly, holding up his ear to catch Nelson's every word.

'I'll do it as if she was, like you, Charley, a bolter, with a ten-pounder offered for her apprehension by her missis in the newspapers,' said Nelson.

'Go on,' said Roberts, impatiently.

'Name, Harcourt,' said Nelson. 'Ship, *Lady Jane Grey*; trade or calling, emigrant; age, twenty-two or twenty-three; height, five feet seven; hair, dark brown; eyes, hazel; nose, slightly curved; mouth, small, with white teeth; complexion, fair, but pale; long, thin neck; and very small ears. Walks remarkably erect; wears on little finger of left hand a white carnelian set in gold, and on third finger of ditto a pearl ring as a guard to wedding ring. Has a habit of saying "You are very kind" to anybody who does anything for her.'

'Hold!' cried Roberts, his bosom swelling with the hope that Emily's presence in Australia might be of service to him. 'Where is she to be found?'

'How much can you stand?' said Nelson, refilling his pipe.

'I have only thirty shillings about me,' said Roberts, 'but *she* has money, and you shall not complain of my want of liberality, Sam.'

CHAPTER XI

GEORGE FLOWER WAS a great character in the colony of New South Wales. He had been transported for discharging, in cold blood, the contents of a double-barrelled gun into the body of a young squire who had seduced his sister. This misfortune had overtaken Flower when he was only nineteen years of age. He was the son of a gamekeeper; and a handsomer lad had rarely breathed. Flower had received a conditional pardon from the Colonial Government for capturing, single-handed, three desperate bushrangers, for whose apprehension a reward of one hundred pounds had been offered in the *Government Gazette*. Flower was now a 'sworn constable', and as a thief-taker was without a rival in the colony. So many attempts had been made upon his life that, like Macbeth, Flower used to boast of having a charmed existence. His sagacity was on a par with his courage and personal prowess; and in many points he strikingly resembled the bloodhound. He walked about the police office in Sydney with a swagger which spoke a consciousness of his superiority in his profession. He was a hard drinker, but liquor rarely had any effect upon him – that is to say, it never interfered with the exercise of his faculties. Although he made a great deal of money by capturing runaways and claiming rewards, Flower was always (to use his own phrase) 'without enough to pay turnpike for a walking stick'. Like some other men in much loftier positions, his 'attachments' were too numerous and too transitory to admit of his living within his means. He had no fixed residence, but was generally 'to be found' about sunset, at a public house kept by a Jew, called Pollack, immediately opposite to the police office. Flower was just on the point of proceeding to Paramatta when Nelson approached him, and said, 'Mr. Flower, I want to speak to you.'

No great man was ever more easy of access than George Flower, and no one more popular with informers, for he invariably acted 'on the square'. His word was his bond; and he never made a promise, either to do a favour for a friend, or bring about an enemy's ruin, without completing it to the very letter. After hearing what Nelson had to say, Flower ordered his horse to be put into the stable, and invited Nelson to have a little dinner with him. It was a prominent feature in Flower's character that he had no petty pride – none of that vulgar prejudice which most emancipated constables entertained against men in an *actual* state of bondage. It must also be mentioned that no informer dared to name his price for putting Flower upon a scent. His terms were well known: half-a-crown out of every pound.

'He has only been out a short time, you see,' said Flower, confidentially, 'and at present he's hardly worth having – £10 from his master, and £5 from the government. Are you quite sure he would never grow into a bushranger, and be worth *fifty* from the government, besides a ticket to anybody that wanted it – yourself, for instance?'

'Never,' said Nelson.

'What was he "lagged" for?' said Flower.

'Forgery,' said Nelson.

'*Oh!*' groaned Flower. 'Then there's no hope of his taking to powder and shot. Forgery! I never knew a forger that was worth his salt. Forgery! Perjury! Larceny! Bigamy! All those crimes ending in 'y' ought to be made death, and no reprieve. Why they send such fellows out here, I don't know. What were *you* lagged for?'

'Stealing,' said Nelson.

'Stealing! Under what circumstances?' said Flower. 'Don't speak false. I can find out, you know, in five minutes.'

Nelson detailed the particulars of his offence, and Flower contemplated him with a searching look of scorn and contempt.

'I hate a thief!' exclaimed George Flower, loudly to himself; but suddenly recollecting that Nelson had just confessed himself one, he said, in an apologetic tone, 'I beg your pardon. Have another glass of whisky.'

It was finally arranged that Nelson was to convey Roberts to Emily's cottage, and leave him there, at a quarter to eleven o'clock.

CHAPTER XII

IT WAS A bleak night in July – the depth of the Australian winter. The wind blew keenly from the south, lifting a hard, gritty dust, which battered the faces of those who attempted to make headway against it. It was ten o'clock, and the convict Roberts, at the corner of the marketplace, anxiously waited for Nelson, who was to conduct him to the cottage where his wretched wife had taken up her abode. Roberts heard footsteps, and trembled lest they should be those of some constable who might take him into custody. He walked stealthily to the other side of the street to wait for the subdued whistle, which it was understood Nelson was to give as the signal of the coast being clear.

Presently Roberts heard that whistle, and neared his shipmate. Nelson, having taken from Roberts every farthing that he had about him, led the way. When they arrived at Emily's cottage, Roberts leaped over the palings and looked through the crevices of the shutters. Emily was seated at the table, reading her bible previous to retiring for the night.

'All right, Sam, it *is* her,' said Roberts to Nelson.

'Am I your friend, or am I not?' asked Nelson.

'You are,' said Roberts. 'Off with you!'

Nelson obeyed him, and in another moment was out of sight. Roberts tapped at the shutter, and Emily, alarmed, inquired, 'Who is there?'

'It's *me*, Emmy darling! It is your Reginald, dearest!' said Roberts, in a low voice. 'Open the door, my own dear Emmy!'

Emily recognised the voice; but she could not believe her ears. 'Who is there?' she again demanded, to satisfy herself; and she placed her ear close to the window.

'Reginald, my love – your own Reginald!' said the convict. 'Don't make a noise, dearest; open the door.'

Emily's doubts were at once dispelled. She flew to the door, unlocked it, and beheld once more her husband! Under other circumstances, his altered appearance – his costume, his sunburnt face and hands, his shabby clothes – would have struck her forcibly; but just then, when she was in the arms of the man to whom she had given herself in passionate and confiding love, she was so overcome with the feeling of joy that they had once more met on the face of the earth, that she clung to him as fondly as she did on the day when she became his bride.

'Tell me, dearest Reginald,' said Emily, 'tell me the truth – do not be offended with me for questioning you – but do, with your own dear lips, assure me that you have not been guilty of the crime they impute to you; tell me truly, Reginald.'

'I am as innocent, Emily, as your own dear self,' said Roberts; and he called upon the Almighty to witness his assertion.

'And you are not Charles Roberts? You are my own Reginald Harcourt? It is false that you are an impostor?'

'False as hell!' said Roberts, theatrically.

'Thank heaven!' exclaimed Emily, clinging to her husband and falling on his breast. 'Oh, Reginald, I am so happy. Never mind, dearest, our present troubles. Truth in the end is sure to prevail. For some wise purpose, Reginald, it is ordained that we should bear this awful reverse of fortune, and let us bear it as cheerfully as we best can. Oh! Reginald—'

At this moment George Flower, who had contrived to secrete himself in Emily's bedroom, whence he overheard all that had passed between the convict and his wife, broke upon the scene – not abruptly, but in the quietest manner possible. Having gently opened the door, he raised a pistol and brought 'the sight' to bear on Roberts's breast. He remained in that position until he had caught Roberts's eye, when he called out, 'If you move hand or foot, you are a dead man! Stand as you are!'

Roberts stood aghast; and Emily, terrified to the last degree, sank into an oak armchair. Speechless, she beheld what followed.

With his eyes, which were like those of an eagle, firmly fixed, and with his forefinger on the trigger of the pistol, Flower slowly approached Roberts. 'Bolter!' said George Flower. 'You know the penalty of even putting your hand into your pocket.' Gradually he came within arm's length of his victim, who stood pale and agitated. Suddenly Flower sprang upon Roberts and secured his hands, and in another instant his wrists were in a pair of brightly polished handcuffs.

'Now then, by your leave, I'll go through the usual form,' said Flower. 'You need not be alarmed, madam,' he added, turning to Emily, 'but I really must pick his pockets – first, of his handkerchief,' he continued, spreading it on the table, 'secondly, of a— Oh! Ah! You *did* happen to have a little pistol about you, did you? Is it loaded?'

'No!' said Roberts, feebly.

'Thirdly, of a pipe, and fourthly, of a small tin box, containing— Eh? What? Oh, you artful! You owdacious lifer! A certificate of freedom, eh? Who have you robbed of this, I wonder? Why, it describes you exactly! How's that? Hulloa! Why, you must have been up to your old tricks again? This is uncommon *like* old Secretary Macleay's signature, but hang me if it *is* his – no, it can't be. I say, how comes the watermark on the paper to be of later date than the pardon itself? Well, while you were about it, you might have seen to that, I think. A small tin box' – Flower passed back to the inventory – 'containing a forged certificate of freedom. Why, this alone would hang you,' argued Flower, 'and as I cannot afford to lose you yet, I'll put it into the fire, and say nothing about it.'

Roberts involuntarily thanked Flower for this net of grace. Emily knelt down and prayed, but the words she uttered were inaudible.

'There's no need of giving this little pistol to the government,' said Flower. 'It's a pretty little thing.' He placed the weapon in his waistcoat pocket, with a complacent smile. 'Then that reduces the property found on the prisoner's person to this handkerchief and this pipe. Well, that will not hurt you, anyhow. Have you got any money?'

'Not a farthing,' said Roberts.

'Well, I'll put a shilling and a few coppers into the handkerchief,' said Flower, 'just to make an appearance in the court, and show that you are not a desperate character. It will look suspicious (for me) if I find *no* money upon you.' These preliminaries arranged, Flower was about to lead Roberts to the nearest cells, and there lock him up, when Emily fell upon her knees. Flower's iron heart was touched by her tears, and gladly would he have relinquished the reward, and set the convict at liberty, had he dared to do so.

'He shall be treated with the greatest kindness and consideration, for your sake, madam,' said Flower. 'It shall not go hard with him: that I promise you.'

'Oh, thank you, thank you!' cried Emily. 'Ah, sir, if you only knew how cruelly he has been treated you would have pity on *him*, as well as on me.'

'You may depend upon me,' said Flower, in a kind and soothing voice. 'Tomorrow I will come and bring you good news. Make yourself quite easy, madam. Good night. Come along, Charley.' He turned to Roberts. 'I've a comfortable bed and a hot supper, and a bottle of port wine, all ready for you at my house.'

~

Flower had not walked more than twenty paces with Roberts, when he pulled up beside a lamppost – one of the very few in that lonely street – and by the dim light he looked peeringly into the convict's hazel eyes.

'I have a precious good mind,' said Flower, 'to take your handcuffs off, and blow your brutal brains out. I'll swear I did it to prevent your escaping. It could be done,' he added, with a movement of the head which convinced Roberts, not only of the practicability of the measure, but of the earnestness of the man who contemplated it.

'Oh, don't, for God's sake! It would break my wife's heart! Why should you shoot me?' said Roberts.

'To rid that beautiful and amiable lady of such a villain as you – to make her free of the crime, the curse, of belonging to such a diabolical scoundrel.'

'Oh, pray don't! You would not murder me in cold blood, surely?' said Roberts, growing more and more alarmed, as he watched the action of George Flower's mouth.

'Murder!' cried Flower. 'That would not be murder. It would be praiseworthy homicide – an act of mercy towards one of God's fairest creatures. I could forgive your forgeries, your thefts, your anything else; but what business had you to marry a lady like that – to link her to your felonies, and then deceive her by calling God to witness your innocence? I heard you, you dog, tell her those falsehoods. Had she a brother?'

'No,' said Roberts.

'Then let me take off those handcuffs,' said Flower, 'and I'll fancy myself her brother. If you attempt to run away, I'll send a bullet through you.'

'Oh, pray don't,' said Roberts. 'Pray, Mr. Flower, don't strike me.'

His entreaties were in vain. Flower unscrewed the handcuffs, and leisurely thrashed Roberts to the cells, where he locked him up in the coldest and most uncomfortable apartment he could find.

CHAPTER XIII

EMILY'S WRONGS HAD filled the mind of the lion-hearted thief-taker. He could not rest. Late as it was, he saddled his horse (Sheriff), and galloped to the cottage to give Emily some good advice. He tapped at the window, and said, 'Throw a cloak on, Mrs. Harcourt, and let me speak to you. I am Flower – George Flower, who was here a little while ago. Don't be frightened, Mrs. Harcourt.'

Emily, who had not retired, opened the door and allowed Flower to enter the cottage.

'You must be very careful in this country, Mrs. Harcourt,' said Flower. 'They are a queer set of people. You must not leave your shutters unbolted, or you'll be robbed, and murdered, perhaps. I got in without any sort of difficulty, while you were reading here, all alone. Tomorrow night I'll send a man down to protect you, and if you lose anything he shall be answerable for it.'

'Oh, you are very kind, Mr. Flower,' said Emily, 'very kind.'

'Don't mention it, madam,' said George, his eyes filling with tears. 'I'd part with my heart's blood to serve you; for you remind me of the days of my boyhood, when my father was Lord Waldane's gamekeeper, and the young ladies used to come down to the Lodge, and talk to my mother and my sister, and sometimes to me. Ah, Mrs. Harcourt, we were as happy a family as any in all England, until a young gentleman – one that I used to go shooting with, and was like a brother to – came and talked of love to my sister Bessy, and robbed her of her honour and her virtue. I couldn't stand it, Mrs. Harcourt. I took his life, and they transported me for it!'

'Dear me!' cried Emily. 'I have often heard the story, and heard you pitied. It happened near Yewbray Bridge.'

'It did so,' said Flower, elated at the idea that the deed had become notorious. 'It did, madam; I am the man. It was not a crime, or I should have repented of it before now, instead of glorying in it, as I did and do. Do you know the country about Yewbray, Mrs. Harcourt?'

'Yes; my father's estate joins that of Lord Waldane, of whom you spoke,' said Emily.

'Indeed!' said Flower, looking at her reverentially.

'My father was member for the county at that time – Mr. Orford; you may have heard of him,' said Emily.

Flower rose from the chair on which Emily had politely requested him to sit down. He contemplated her with curiosity, pity, and respect. He could not speak for several minutes, but tears, and they were scalding hot, chased each other so rapidly down his cheeks that they dropped from his chin upon the floor.

'You the daughter of Mr. Orford!' exclaimed Flower, when his voice was restored to him. 'You the daughter of Mr. Orford – the gentleman who saved my life by going to the Home Secretary on my behalf. You know I was cast for death. *You* here, in this accursed jail! *You* the wife of a man transported for life! You in Botany Bay! This is a strange world, but I never expected to witness a scene like this!' The thief-taker went down upon his knees, and with the fingers which had long been used to roughly handle the most desperate criminals, he gently pressed, with the spirit of an idolator, the feet of the wretched woman, who shrank at the thought of being alone with, and touched by, a man who had taken the life of a fellow creature.

'I will repay the kindness your father showed to me when he came to see me in the condemned cells, with heavy chains upon me, boy as I then was,' said Flower. 'I can do anything I like in this country, Mrs. Harcourt. They say I am the greatest man in this large island, and I believe I am. Members of council, and magistrates, when they meet me, pull up and say, "Well, George, how are you?" There's nothing that I can't do. I might own thousands upon thousands of acres of land, and flocks of sheep, and herds of cattle, as big as Macarthur's or Wentworth's, and I might have lots of ships in the harbour, like Cooper and Wright; but what use would they all be to me, when I can't get rid of that thought which is always uppermost in my brain? Why had not that man that I killed five hundred thousand lives, instead of one, for me to take? I mean the man that seduced my sister Bessy. She was a dear girl, and very good looking, and gentle, and nice spoken, and oh!, so like *you*, that you might have been sisters.'

'Be kind to my unfortunate husband,' said Emily, in reply to this impassioned harangue. 'Be kind to poor Reginald, Mr. Flower.'

'I will,' returned Flower. 'But don't say *Mister* – it feels so cold and distant. Say *George*, do this, or do that, and it shall be done.'

'Have my husband restored to me,' said Emily. 'I care not how frugally and humbly we may live, but all I want is to be with my husband. I want to be alone with my husband.'

'It shall be done,' said Flower. 'I, who have the power of life and death constantly in my hands – I, George Flower, say it shall be done; but you must wait for a fortnight.'

CHAPTER XIV

FLOWER DID NOT overestimate his influence, when he informed Emily of its extent. By fair means or by foul, there was nothing, seemingly, that George could not do. In the police office he exercised supreme power, albeit he was in a subordinate position; and 'amongst the gentry of New South Wales' there was scarcely a person who was not under some obligation to him, either for recovering cattle, horses, or other property that had been stolen, or for apprehending bushrangers who infested the roads between Sydney and their estates. Mr. Dawson, Roberts's master, had a particular regard for George Flower. He had on one occasion been an eyewitness of Flower's wonderful coolness and bravery, when a gang of convicts rebelled, knocked out the brains of sundry overseers, and set authority at defiance.

When Flower left Emily, he returned to the cells where Roberts was locked up. With a very bad grace, he gave directions that Roberts should have a bed to lie upon, a plate to eat his victuals from, and some tobacco now and then, if he wanted to smoke.

'Don't speak to me, you villain,' said Flower to Roberts, when the latter returned thanks for the former's kindness. 'Don't look at me, even, or I'll spoil your beauty, you white-livered, black-hearted, pettifogging*, filthy-minded, double-distilled essence of a cowardly, cringing, woman-deceiving criminal. You are a nice fellow to represent yourself as an officer and a gentleman!' Hereupon he seized Roberts by the left ear, and pinched it savagely.

'Let him be taken into court at ten o'clock this morning, Johnson, and remanded for a week,' said Flower, to a brother constable. 'Tell the magistrate I will give my deposition as soon as I come back from Campbell Town.'

'All right,' returned Johnson. 'Is he worth anything?'

'No, the beast; only £10,' said Flower. 'And here am I with a ride of thirty miles there and thirty back before me.'

~

It would be difficult to say which of the two was superior in the endurance of fatigue, and in abstinence from sleep and food – George Flower or his little horse, Sheriff.

Sheriff was not more than thirteen hands high, and Flower was not less than twelve stone; and yet they had frequently been seen together at Sydney in the morning, and at Bong Bong at night – the distance between the two places being one hundred and four miles, the road a very bad one, and several rivers and broad streams to wade through or swim across.

Sheriff had shared many of his master's dangers, and bore the marks upon his compact body. When the famous Donahough, from behind a huge ironbark tree, upon the Liverpool Road, discharged from an old Tower musket a handful of swan shot, at the distance of eighty yards, at George Flower, Sheriff received a goodly number of

---

* Roberts had been an articled clerk to an attorney.

them in his left shoulder, and one in his left eye, which destroyed the sight thereof. On another occasion, a bullet, which broke George Flower's arm, had struck Sheriff on the near quarter, and left a large mark; but, to use Flower's own words, 'He never said a word, but stood like a stone, as if he enjoyed a lark of that sort.' And there was a small piece out of Sheriff's right ear. That, too, had been lost in an engagement with the enemy.

Onward jogged Flower and Sheriff, as jauntily as though there was no danger to be met with on the road. The huge pockets of Flower's fustian shooting coat contained each a large pistol, and several pairs of handcuffs; and in each waistcoat pocket there was a small weapon, besides the one which had been taken from Roberts. In his trousers' pockets were sundry rounds of ball cartridge, and a clasp knife, with which Flower had been 'compelled to hamstring two of the gang' whom he caught in the bush near Prospect – 'the one a fifty pounder, and the other a twenty-fiver', besides 'a sweat at the silver swag', which 'they had just taken from two harmless gents, who had come out free from England to buy sheep and cattle, and turn farmers, and all that sort of thing'.

Flower considered it a part of his duty to enter every public house on the road; and in the days we write of, they were about four or five miles apart. Out of compliment to the landlord, he always drank something.

With all the barmaids Flower was a prodigious favourite; he was always so lively and pleasant in his conversation – so kind and gentle in his manners, but invariably so respectful and modest in his demeanour. No being in this world was ever more completely under the influence of the softer sex than George Flower. After inflicting summary punishment on a prisoner, and using the strongest language in the verandah of a public house, he would approach a female at the bar, and talk to her in a strain which was frequently refined and sentimental. With young children he was a perfect child himself. He would encourage them to pull his hair and whiskers, beat him with his own whip, which he would put into their tiny hands, give them a ride on Sheriff, or chase the fowls and ducks round the yard for their especial amusement.

CHAPTER XV

'WHAT! FLOWER!' EXCLAIMED Mr. Dawson, on George riding up and touching his straw hat to him.

'Good morning, sir,' said Flower. 'I happened to have a little business in this quarter, and thought I'd just look in and say how do ye do, as I was passing.'

'I'm delighted to see you,' said Mr. Dawson. 'Get off, and send the little horse round to the stables for a feed of corn, and come in and have a glass of porter and a pipe, and tell me of your adventures.'

'Not many to tell, sir,' said Flower. 'There is not a really good placard on the walls – tens, and fifteens, and twenties; but not a single three-figure gentleman' – he meant £100 – 'among 'em. By the way, Mr. Dawson, there's a little money of yours in the market, I see.'

'Yes, George, and I wish you could finger it,' said Mr. Dawson. 'He is hardly worth *your* while, but if you could lay hold of him, I'd be very much obliged to you, and besides the £10 you should have any colt or filly out of the two-year-old batch. I am very anxious to have that man apprehended.'

'Why, has he been and done anything besides running away?' asked Flower.

'Done?' cried Mr. Dawson. 'He has spoilt the whole of my assigned servants. Made them discontented and bad men. Caused them to complain of me to the nearest bench of magistrates. I have been represented as a master who limes their flour, and feeds them on shins of beef instead of wholesome flesh, and as one who works them to death. Before that fellow came here, I had not occasion for three years to get a man punished; and *since* he came, almost every man has either been flogged or put upon the treadmill.'

'I know you are a good master,' said Flower. 'But tell me, Mr. Dawson, how did you employ this runaway?'

'Why, I used to set him to shell Indian corn, skim the cream off the milk bowls, drive the parrots out of the wheat fields, feed the pigs, and on baking days, attend to the fire in the oven, and all such light and easy jobs I used to give him, for he had never been accustomed to hard work, and could not do it; it blistered his hands.'

'Why didn't you break him in to bullock driving?' said Flower.

'Because I pitied the blackguard at first.'

'Ah! Pity's a dangerous thing in this country, Mr. Dawson,' said Flower. 'A little of it ought to go a very long way. I've known many a promising young man ruined by pity. Now, sir, suppose I was to get a scent of this Roberts and arouse him from his slumbers by rattling these handcuffs in his ears, what would you do with him after he was punished?'

'Turn him in to Government.'

'Don't do that sir. Look here, Mr. Dawson,' said Flower. 'I applied to Gov'ment the other day for a servant, who turns out to be a tailor. He made these clothes I've got on, and very well made they are. But of tailors in Sydney there's a regular glut, and my tailor cannot earn more than nine and sixpence a week, out of which I take seven shillings. Now, your lawyer – I know he's a lawyer – would be able to earn at least a pound a week, copying papers and all that sort of thing; and by keeping a tight hand over him I could turn the fellow to good account. Why not make a swop? You have got a lot of men, and you might buy duck and cloth, and let this tailor be always employed, instead of buying ready-made slops in the market. To tell you the honest truth, I have got Roberts in my possession, and have come here to talk about him; never mind the filly and the £10, give me the man and take the tailor, and I'll be satisfied. The papers can be got ready in the office, and Gov'ment's sanction I'll procure by the time he's dealt with.'

Mr. Dawson accepted Flower's proposal, and the business being concluded, George saddled Sheriff and returned to Sydney. He went at once to Emily's cottage, where he found her in great grief. Her writing desk had been stolen, and it contained all the money she had in the world, besides several little trinkets which were very precious in her sight.

'Don't let this distress you,' said Flower, after a few minutes' reflection. 'You shall have it back tonight.'

'Pray sit down,' said Emily. 'You look very tired.'

'No, Mrs. Harcourt, I will not sit down,' said Flower.

'Will Reginald be restored to me?'

'Yes.'

'God bless you!' cried Emily. 'You are indeed a kind friend to me.'

Flower cantered Sheriff down to Mrs. White's house, and called out, 'Nelson'.

Nelson came.

'I want to talk to you, my boy, about Roberts,' said Flower. 'Just come into the Barrack Square with me. I'll leave my horse at these palings.'

Nelson, who was flattered by this condescension, accompanied Flower into the Barrack Square.

'I say, where's that writing desk?' said Flower, when they were alone.

'What writing desk?' said Nelson.

'*That* writing desk,' said Flower, striking Nelson on the bridge of the nose a blow which swelled up both his eyes and felled him to the earth. '*That* writing desk,' repeated Flower, placing the thick sole of his boot upon Nelson's neck. 'Gurgle up the receiver, or I'll squeeze out your poisonous existence.'

'Abrahams!' gasped Nelson.

'If ever you steal *that* writing desk again,' said Flower, leaving Nelson on the ground, writhing in pain from the kicks he had received, 'I'll give you such a thrashing as you will not forget in a hurry.'

CHAPTER XVI

WHEN FLOWER LEFT Nelson, he directed his steps towards the police office, where he provided himself with a 'jemmy', an instrument used by burglars for effecting an entrance. Thus armed, he hastened to the residence of Mr. Isaac Abrahams, an old Jew, who had been transported to the colony so far back as Governor Bligh's administration.

Mr. Isaac Abrahams was very rich; he had become so by being engaged in various occupations – to wit, receiving stolen property, lending money at usurious rates of interest, crimping, dealing in second-hand clothes, and keeping for many years a public house in that part of the town of Sydney which is frequented by sailors – a place called 'The Rocks'.

Abrahams and his wife were in bed when Flower arrived at their dwelling. Without any sort of ceremony, Flower inserted the 'jemmy' into a window shutter, which he wrenched from its hinges. He then broke a pane of glass, put his hand through the aperture, drew the bolt, lifted the sash, and vaulted into Abrahams's dining parlour.

The Jew heard the noise, got out of bed, and called aloud, 'Who's there?'

'It's only me, Ikey,' cried Flower. 'You need not come

down. I am coming up. It's only me – George Flower, Ikey.'

In another moment Flower was in the Jew's bedroom.

'By heaven! Mr. Flower, what do you mean?' cried the Jew. 'Why do you come into my bedroom? At this hour of night, too!'

'On business, Ikey.'

'Then why do you come like a thief, breaking into the house? Couldn't you knock at the door?'

'No, Ikey. Fish up that writing box you fenced this afternoon!'

'Are you mad, Mr. Flower?'

'No, Ikey; but you must be. To think that a man of your time of life, with all your money, should go putting your neck into the noose for a paltry thing like that. To think that you shouldn't be able to leave off your old tricks after you've made your fortune! Forbes' – Flower always spoke of the Chief Justice in this familiar manner – 'would lag you to Norfolk Island for life for fencing that box.'

'What box?'

'Now, none of your nonsense. I can't stop here all night. And if I have to search for it, and find it, I'll take both you and the box away together.'

'Take a glass of spirits-and-water, Mr. Flower,' said the Jew, blandly.

'Well, I will,' said Flower, 'on the lid of that writing box; fish both the box and the grog up at one dive – they are both in this room.'

The Jew opened an iron chest, in which he kept the title deeds of lands mortgaged to him, bonds, promissory and bank notes – jewels, gold, silver, and other valuables; and from this chest the Jew reluctantly brought out the writing desk that Nelson had that day stolen from Emily's bedroom. He then produced a case bottle and a tumbler, which Flower half filled with liquor.

'Ikey,' said Flower, after he had refreshed himself with the gin, 'I am awfully hard up. Lend us a flimsy. I don't want to be hard with you, Ikey. Make it a fifty, for which I give you my verbal promissory note, payable with interest.'

'Mr. Flower,' said the Jew, 'I always had a great respect for you, and I've often felt sorry that you didn't belong to our persuasion.'

'Don't flatter me, Ikey,' said Flower, 'or you'll make me vain, and vanity is a bad thing; so stump up the money, and let me go.'

The Jew again visited the iron chest, and produced a bank note for £50. Having satisfied himself that it was not a bad one, Flower returned to Emily's cottage, which was not very far distant from where the Jew then lived.

CHAPTER XVII

THE NEXT DAY Roberts was placed at the bar of the police office. Flower appeared in court, and made a deposition to the following effect: 'I, George Flower, police constable, hereby make oath and say that this deponent met the prisoner at the bar in a house in Castlereagh Street, on the night of the 26th instant; that this deponent took the prisoner into custody, and found upon his person a pocket-handkerchief and a pipe, here produced; that this deponent, after apprehending the prisoner, who is an assigned servant of Mr. Dawson of Campbell Town, proceeded to his master, and inquired whether he had any charge to bring forward against him, beyond that of absconding from his employ, and this deponent states that the said Mr. Dawson told this deponent that he had no charge whatever to bring forward against the prisoner in this court.'

'Did he make any resistance, Flower?' inquired the magistrate.

'None whatever, your worship,' said Flower.

'I suppose fifty lashes would do for him?' said the magistrate.

'I don't think he could stand fifty,' said Flower. 'The mill and the Carter's Barracks crop would suit his circumstances better, your worship, *I* think. As he has never run away before, seven days, perhaps, would be a sufficient lesson.'

Roberts was accordingly sentenced to seven days on the treadmill, and was forthwith removed to Carter's Barracks, where, preparatory to entering upon his punishment, his hair was cut as closely as possible with a pair of very sharp shears.

Flower made an excuse to Emily for her husband's absence, by saying that he had gone up to Campbell Town to get his clothes from Mr. Dawson's; and meanwhile Flower negotiated 'the transfer'.

When Roberts came 'off the mill', Flower went down to Carter's Barracks to receive him. 'Halloa, Captain!' cried he. 'You are now my assigned servant, and I'm going to leave you down at that house in Castlereagh Street, just to look after the premises. Come along.'

While they were walking down the road, Flower harangued Roberts: 'Don't suppose, you miserable thief,' he thus began, 'that you are going to lead a life of idleness. Quite the contrary. I intend to make you work. I shall let you out to an attorney for three pound a week, and if ever you absent yourself from office – and I shall keep a sharp lookout upon you – I'll dust your jacket with this cane, and you know how it makes you tingle, don't you?' And fearing that Roberts's memory might be treacherous on this head, he gave him several smart blows on the calves of his legs, which made the convict dance in the street and cry for mercy. 'And if ever you say one word to your wife of how I serve you,' said Flower, 'you'll be missing some fine morning, and no one will ever hear anything more about you. By the bye, what plausible reason can you assign to your wife for that blacking brush condition of your infamous poll, you pettifogging blackguard, you?'

'I'll say I had a stroke of the sun,' said Roberts, 'and was obliged to get my head shaved the other day.'

'Capital!' cried Flower. 'If I'd known you'd have been so ready as that, I'd have spared you that last stroke of the cane which I gave you just now. There's another thing I wish to say,' continued Flower. 'Never ask your wife for money, and if she offers you any, don't take it. If I find you disobeying me in this, I'll flog you within an inch of your life. And don't allow any of your acquaintances ever to come inside the house where your wife is – do you hear? And see that the garden is weeded with your own hands, and everything kept in proper order. I shall come down pretty often, just to see how you're getting on, you know. You understand me?'

'Oh, yes,' said Roberts. 'And I'm very much obliged to you, Mr. Flower, and you'll find that my conduct will be most exemplary, I assure you, and in the end you will discover that I have not been, and that I am not, anything like so bad as you at present conceive.'

'I don't wish to have any of your talk,' returned Flower. 'And as for my kindness to you, I give you to understand that you're under no obligations to me whatsoever. I tell you plainly that if I had my will, I'd hang you this very day.'

CHAPTER XVIII

FLOWER HIRED OUT Roberts, as he threatened, to an attorney, at a salary of £250 a year, for Roberts, it was discovered, had a very good insight into the art of special pleading and the principles of conveyancing. In short, Roberts was a very clever fellow, and could do an immense deal of work, when he was so disposed, in a very short time. His salary was drawn every week by Flower, and duly handed over to Emily, who increased this income by giving lessons in music and dancing.

Roberts had provided himself with becoming apparel, and his external appearance once more resembled that of a gentleman. Although Flower hated him with the same intensity as ever, he had nevertheless no fault to find with him, and was rejoiced beyond measure to see Emily so happy and so comfortable in her small abode.

At the end of three months, Roberts began to grow weary of leading a steady and virtuous life. He was sorely afraid of Flower, while he continued Flower's assigned servant; and did not dare to indulge in the slightest irregularity so long as he was owned by so firm and powerful a master. He therefore begged Emily to request Flower to transfer him to herself, and thus make him his own wife's assigned servant.

~

One evening, when Flower went down to visit Mrs. Harcourt (although Roberts was called by his proper name, his wife continued to be called Mrs. Harcourt), she proposed this transfer of her husband.

'My dear madam,' said Flower, 'it would end in your own misery. What hold, I should like to know, would *you* have upon him?'

'What hold!' cried Emily. 'What stronger hold can there be than my affection for him, and his affection for me? Ah! George Flower, you don't know dear Reginald! If you only knew what a kind, good, generous, noble-minded, single-hearted creature he really is, you would not think so harshly of him as you now seem to do.'

'My dear madam,' returned Flower, 'I know that your husband is all that you have described him; but in my opinion it would be as well if matters were allowed to stand as they now are. See how happy you are! What more can you desire?'

'Yes, it is very true, George, and I ought to be, and I am, very grateful indeed, for all your goodness to me, and to my unfortunate, innocent Reginald; but oh! If you would grant me this request!' said Emily.

'I tell you it would be the worst thing in the world, Mrs. Harcourt,' said Flower. 'Do you suppose I should refuse, or make any objection, if I thought it would be to your advantage? Now, take my advice; do not press this any further.'

But Emily had promised her husband that she *would* press it.

'Ah, you were never so obstinate before,' she began. 'Of late you seem quite changed.'

'Obstinate!' exclaimed Flower. 'Obstinate! I'd go through fire and brimstone to do you a service; but to grant what you now ask would be downright madness.'

'Then you mean to tell me that dear Reginald is not to be trusted?'

'No, I do not say that.'

'Then what can be your objection?'

'It would be unlucky.'

'Unlucky! Ah! You are trifling with me.' Emily's eyes filled with tears.

Flower's heart was again touched, and he immediately agreed to the proposition, expressing his sorrow that he had refused her in the first instance.

Roberts came home shortly after this, and Flower presently asked him to look at a horse which he said he was about to buy.

'And so you wish to be transferred to your wife, do you? Oh, how I should like to break your bones!' said Flower, when they were out of Emily's hearing.

'It is her own wish, I assure you, on my honour,' said Roberts.

'On your *honour*!' said Flower, and he kicked Roberts several times.

'I assure you it is her own thought, her own wish,' Roberts repeated.

In his violent anger Flower lost his presence of mind, and instead of beating Roberts, as was his wont, in such a way as to leave no visible marks, he struck him a heavy blow in the face, which laid open Roberts's upper lip.

Roberts took out his lawn pocket-handkerchief, and applied it to his mouth, which was now bleeding profusely.

'Turn upon me, you contemptible forger, you thief!' cried Flower. 'Turn upon me – strike me – throw a stone at me, *do* – do something that will justify me in pounding the breath out of your dastardly body!'

'Strike my deliverer, my benefactor?' said Roberts. 'No, Mr. Flower, whatever may be my sins, I am not ungrateful.'

'Oh, heaven!' groaned Flower. 'And things like you are called men! Now, don't look at me in that cringing way, or I'll gouge both your eyes out, I will. My blood is up, and I am thirsting to avenge the wrongs of that lady by tearing you to pieces.' And with these words Flower gnashed his teeth, and seized Roberts by the hair, and shook him with the boisterous ferocity of an excited fiend. 'I'll be in at your death yet,' gasped Flower, exhausted by passion. 'I will. I feel it. I will! I will! I will!'

CHAPTER XIX

FLOWER ABSTAINED FROM visiting Emily for several days. He intended to keep his promise, but wished to delay doing so until the last moment. Besides, Flower was not quite satisfied that Roberts would, on this occasion, conceal from Emily the rough handling to which he had been subjected; and this formed an additional reason for staying away. At length Emily wrote to Flower, and begged him to come and see her, as she had something very particular to say to him. It was curious to observe the sudden changes in the expression of Flower's countenance when he read Emily's note. At first a very pleasing smile – a smile which was called up by affectionate regard and pity – played over his fine bold features; then came a scowl and compressed lips, while his eyes seemed to flash fire; and then, when he again looked at Emily's handwriting, the kind smile returned, speedily followed by that awful, ay, diabolical look.

It was just as Flower expected. The 'something very particular' was the 'transfer'. Flower went down upon his knees and implored her to forego her demand, and passionately, but tenderly, uplifting his hands, assured her that she was asking him to sign the warrant for Roberts's ruin and her own eternal wretchedness. 'Mrs. Harcourt!' he exclaimed. 'Must I tell you the truth? Yes, you drive me to do so. Your husband is not what you think him, not what you have described him to be. His outside is like that of a gentleman; but within he is low, and tainted with the ideas and habits that belong only to the very dregs of mankind.'

'Mr. Flower!' said Emily, indignantly. 'Do you imagine that Captain Harcourt would deceive me?'

'How can you be so blind, so childishly simple, as to be imposed upon by that man, when the very proofs of his deceit are ever before your eyes?' said Flower. 'Did he not tell you that he was a captain in a dragoon regiment, and that he had never done any work in his life until he came to this country?'

'Nor had he, Mr. Flower.'

'Then how comes it that he is, suddenly, the best lawyer in Sydney? How comes it that, if you will only let him remain as he now is, he shall earn £500 a year, but that if he is freed from my authority he will not earn a shilling himself, but drain you of all your little hard-earned savings to gratify his low and inborn tastes?'

'Mr. Flower!' again cried Emily, indignantly.

'Mrs. Harcourt, hear me!' returned Flower.

'No, Mr. Flower, this is a mere pretext,' said Emily. 'You made me a promise, and now you wish to break it.' She wept and sobbed violently.

'Don't cry, Mrs. Harcourt, don't cry; I cannot stand that,' said Flower. 'I did not mean to hurt your feelings.'

'Then why did you slander poor Reginald? It is hard enough to be convicted when innocent, and sent to this horrid country, and debarred the comforts of his former life, without being vilified in such a dreadful manner.'

'Yes, but don't cry any more,' said Flower.

'As for being suddenly the best lawyer in Sydney,' said Emily, 'why, of course he is. Reginald is so clever that he could learn anything quickly. He would be the best doctor in a month, if he were to study medicine; or the best anything he gave his mind to for a little time. You do not know Reginald, Mr. Flower.'

'I'm afraid I do not,' said Flower.

CHAPTER XX

ONE DAY, WHEN Emily was standing in the little garden in front of her cottage, a gentleman named Brade, one of the police magistrates, happened to pass by, and see her face. Mr. Brade, whose disposition may be described as 'very gay', admired Emily exceedingly, and he passed and re-passed several times, and stared at her. Emily observed this, and retired to the cottage, of which she very rarely crossed the threshold.

Mr. Brade made inquiry, and informed himself who Mrs. Harcourt was, and further discovered what sort of a person her husband was. Mr. Brade's informant also told him of George Flower's acquaintance with the lady, and suggested that it would be advisable to get Flower out of the way, before obtaining an introduction to Mrs. Harcourt.

To get Flower out of the way was far from difficult. There happened to be at large, near Bathurst, three men who had baffled all the efforts of the mounted police. A hundred pounds' reward had been offered for the apprehension of each of them, and Flower had often sighed to take them 'single handed', but he could not make up his mind to leave Emily unprotected, for he was in constant dread lest some person in power should be struck with her beauty, and, in his absence, cause her annoyance.

Mr. Brade, while sitting on the bench, took up the newspaper, the *Australian*, and read the last daring act of the bushrangers.

'Swinton,' said Mr. Brade to the chief magistrate, 'have you seen this?' pointing to the paragraph.

'Yes,' replied the chief magistrate, 'I have just been talking to Major Doole about it.' (Major Doole was also a magistrate, then sitting on the bench.)

'This ought not to be,' said Mr. Brade. 'These men ought to be taken. Let us have a meeting in the private room, and send for George Flower.'

'I have spoken to him already,' said the chief, 'but he does not seem disposed to have a venture. I don't know what has come over George Flower, lately. He is getting lazy and timid, I fancy.'

'Let us all talk to him, and put him upon his mettle,' said Mr. Brade.

At the breaking up of the court, George Flower *was* sent for, and taken into the private room. The three magistrates vied with each other in painting the glory which attached to Flower's past career, and succeeded in inflaming his vanity; but he declined the errand they proposed, on the ground that it was not fair to rob the mounted police of their legitimate profits; besides, he pleaded that he was tired of being made a target, and thought of retiring from the police, and keeping a public house.

'Oh! A thousand pities!' cried Mr. Brade. 'Only fancy – what would the police be without *you*, George Flower? *You* are the police! What are *we*, without *you*? What is the Government without *you*? Nothing! The convicts would take the country from us, if it were not for *you*; for the military could never keep down the convicts without the police, and I repeat that *you* are the police! And if you are bent on keeping a public house, why you would have these three hundred pounds to set you up: one hundred would buy you a cask of rum, another a cask of gin, and the third, a cask of brandy; and then, after such an exploit, the prettiest girls in the country would be dying to marry you. What a finish to your fame it would be!'

'As to the money for setting up a public house,' said Flower, argumentatively, 'I could easily manage that. And as for the pretty girls,' he added, with a smile playing on his lips, 'there is no lack of them. But the fact is, I don't want to go.'

'Come, come, George,' said the chief magistrate, 'undertake it as a personal favour to all of us; and I promise you that if you are successful your *conditional* shall be changed into a *free* pardon.'

'I don't care about a free pardon now,' said Flower. 'I don't want to visit my native land again – I have now an inducement to remain in this country, and I wouldn't go home tomorrow if I could.'

'Ah,' cried Mr. Brade, 'I begin to think, George, you suspect that one of this gang is more than a match for you. They say he is monstrously clever, cunning, and courageous.'

'A match for me, sir!' said Flower. 'I believe there's only one person that's a match for me.' He significantly pointed with his forefinger – insinuating that the person he alluded to was down below. 'However, since you are all so determined upon it, I *will* go, and bring in this clever fellow you speak of – dead in a cart, and t'others tied to the cart's tail – and I'll do it before this day six weeks.'

'Bravo!' cried out the three magistrates. Mr. Brade, in

his ecstasy, held out his hand and shook warmly the small but vigorous fist of the dauntless thief-taker.

Flower that night left Sydney. But before he went on his journey he paid a visit to Emily. He found her in excellent spirits, which were strangely in contrast with his own melancholy frame of mind.

CHAPTER XXI

FLOWER WAS NO sooner out of Sydney than Mr. Brade wrote a very polite note to 'Mr. Roberts', requesting him to call at his private residence. Mr. Brade received Roberts with extreme courtesy, pitied his unfortunate position, expressed his implicit belief in the convict's innocence, and then informed Roberts that he desired his opinion upon a point of law on so delicate a subject that he did not wish to submit it through an attorney to counsel.

Roberts was of course 'highly flattered', and gave Mr. Brade a very sound opinion on the imaginary case which Mr. Brade verbally made known to him; and knowing well where Roberts lived, he inquired what was his address, in order that he might convey to him some sense of the obligation under which he said he was labouring. Roberts without hesitation gave Mr. Brade the number of his house in Castlereagh Street.

On the following morning Mr. Brade called, and presented Roberts with five sovereigns and five shillings, delicately folded up in a piece of silver paper. Whilst he was talking to Roberts, his eye rested upon Emily's piano, and upon a basket containing some Berlin wools.

'You are musical, I perceive,' said Mr. Blade, addressing Roberts in the tone of an equal.

'*I* am not,' replied Roberts, 'but Mrs.——, that is to say, my wife, sometimes amuses herself.' (Roberts just then felt too proud to say that his wife gave lessons.)

'Oh! You are married? I was not aware, or' – he simpered and smiled – 'I should not have thought of calling in so rugged a costume.'

'Oh, pray don't mention that. In this country one does not expect those who have business to attend to should be always attired in the garb of morning visitors.' Roberts went to the door and called out: 'Emily, my love, come downstairs!'

Emily, in obedience to her husband's commands, made her appearance, but much against her inclination, for she had from the window recognised in Mr. Brade the gentleman who had stared so strangely at her on a previous day.

Mr. Brade stayed for several hours, chatting with Roberts and his wife, and on taking his departure he invited them to visit him on the ensuing Sunday, at his villa, a few miles from town upon the South Head Road.

Roberts accepted the invitation; but when Mr. Brade had gone, Emily expressed her regret that he had done so.

Roberts, than whom a more cunning man never breathed, 'saw through' Mr. Brade as quickly as Emily had 'seen through' him; but Roberts was not a jealous man, and as his wife did not breathe her suspicions, he was determined to foster, rather than obstruct, Mr. Brade's desire to become acquainted with them.

'My dear love,' said Roberts, 'it is highly desirable we should be on terms of intimacy with the magistracy. They have the power of recommending persons in my position for pardons, conditional or absolute, as the case may be. Who knows but that Mr. Brade, who is satisfied of my innocence, as you will hear him say yourself on Sunday next – Mr. Brade, a police magistrate, and lately an officer in her Majesty's service, like myself, and on the most intimate terms at Government-House – who knows whether he may not be the means of procuring my return to the land of my fathers, and ample compensation from the Home Government for the wrongs they have inflicted upon me by this unmerited banishment? Mr. Brade, my dear, is not a man like Flower; he is a gentleman, a person of exquisite sensibility and good taste. You see it in his manner, his address, and his conversation. It would be madness, my dear Emily, to spurn the spontaneous advances of a gentleman of his calibre and character.'

Overcome by these arguments, Emily's scruples about visiting Mr. Brade were speedily dissipated.

Sunday came, and Roberts drove Emily in his gig to Mr. Brade's country residence, which overlooked a small branch of the harbour of Port Jackson, called Rose Bay, one of the most lovely spots in the world.

The bay is almost semicircular, and margined by a broad path of cream-white sand. It is so completely shut in that its waters are rarely troubled; and upon this Sunday they were as the surface of an enormous mirror, which reflected the shadows of the trees and rocks skirting this calm expanse of water.

Butterflies were on the wing, and diamond birds were chasing each other from bush to bush; the mockingbirds were singing in the mangrove trees, and from a distance there came upon the ear the low cooings of the bronze-winged pigeon. Heaths of every description were in full flower, but their perfume was drowned by the overpowering scent of the mimosa and the wild laburnum.

After luncheon, Mr. Brade proposed a walk round the bay, and promised to exhibit to Emily, from a certain peak, its transcendent beauties.

They had not proceeded far when Roberts lagged behind, while Mr. Brade and Emily walked leisurely on.

Emily looked behind her several times, and at length stopped, and called to her husband, who was now out of sight, 'Reginald, are you not coming?'

Roberts heard her voice, but gave no reply. He smiled, and smoked more vigorously the cheroot which he had secretly lighted. Roberts was premeditating a return to the villa for the purpose of draining the decanter of its delicious sherry.

Again Emily stopped, and called out, 'Reginald!'

'I am afraid my husband will be lost,' said she to Mr. Brade.

'There is no fear of that,' returned Mr. Brade. 'My good madam, husbands are not such fools.'

At that moment Roberts was acting on his premeditation. He had drank nearly a tumblerful of the wine, and was pouring the like quantity of water into the decanter. He had heard Mr. Brade say, at luncheon, that this was a trick his servants were addicted to, and Roberts concluded that they would have to bear the blame when this impudent dilution was detected by their master, at dinner.

Emily began to feel alarmed, for Mr. Brade's attentions, and the opinions he ventured to express, were offensive to the last degree. She intimated that she had seen sufficient of the beauties of Rose Bay, and would fancy the rest. She then left Mr. Brade's arm, and retraced her steps to the villa, Mr. Brade walking by her side, and paying her the most extravagant compliments.

When they reached the villa, Roberts was walking up and down the verandah, pretending to read a book. When he beheld his wife, flushed with anger, approaching the steps, and Mr. Brade a few paces behind her, he guessed that she had been insulted, but he suffered no species of resentment to ruffle his soul, which had seemingly been convicted with his body, and transported in bondage to a land where both were in subjection to every man in power.

For the first time in her life, Emily was in a passion. She could not suppose that her husband was a party to the insults which had been offered to her, but she thought it was unpardonably *dull* in him not to have perceived that her personal charms (she was quite aware of their extent) were the mainspring of Mr. Brade's civilities.

'What! Are you tired, Emmy, dear?' said Roberts.

'Yes,' she replied, curtly, and walked into a room which had been given up to her.

'My wife never was a good walker,' said Roberts, cringingly.

'So it seems,' replied the magistrate, twirling his moustache.

'She rarely takes any exercise whatever,' said Roberts.

'Ah!' said the magistrate.

'It is very warm today, sir, is it not?' said Roberts.

'Very,' said the magistrate, imperiously, still twirling his moustache. 'I shall drink some wine.' And he called to a servant, 'Bring me some sherry, slave!'

The sherry was brought. As soon as Mr. Brade tasted it, he placed the glass upon the tray, and looked at the servant.

'What is this you have brought me?' he inquired.

'Wine, sir,' said the servant.

'Wine!' Mr. Brade echoed him in a loud voice, which Emily heard. 'Wine! You convicted scoundrel! I'll teach you to put in water into my wine. Go into my bedroom.'

The convict servant obeyed, and presently Mr. Brade followed him.

'What do you mean, sir,' said Mr. Brade, after he had closed the door, 'by watering the wine, when I have guests in the house? It is bad enough to do it when I am alone.'

'Please, sir, I didn't do it,' said the man. 'It was that gentleman. I saw him.'

Emily heard all this, and was shocked at the servant's depravity.

'How dare you tell me such a falsehood?' said Mr. Brade. 'I intended to flog you moderately, but now you shall have it severely.' And forthwith he lashed him with a hunting whip.

The man howled, cried, and implored him to desist. But Mr. Brade, whose passions were now tempestuous, gave no ear to his cries. Emily was afraid that Mr. Brade would flog the man to death, and fain would have interceded on his behalf, sinful as she thought he had been in attempting to put the blame on 'Reginald'; but she did not dare to interfere, although she felt, in her own heart, that the cold reception she had given to Mr. Brade's attentions was intimately connected with the awful severity of the chastisement he was bestowing on his servant.

Exhausted by his labours, Mr. Brade went into the verandah; and, when he had recovered his breath, talked to Roberts.

'If they would content themselves,' said Mr. Brade, 'with stealing a portion, and leaving the rest unspoiled, I could forgive them; but watering one's wine – 'tis abominable.'

'Horrible,' said Roberts. 'I have often felt as you now feel. But what *can* one do with a parcel of low rascals?'

'Flog their backs bare!' cried Mr. Brade.

Roberts, unobserved by Mr. Brade, involuntarily shuddered, and changing the conversation, praised the beauty of the villa and the grounds.

'Who designed them?' inquired Roberts.

'*I* did,' said Mr. Brade.

'You must have exquisite taste in architecture.'

'Yes, I have studied the art very attentively for years.'

'And the result has repaid you. I never beheld anything so perfect. Even the site on which you have built the villa. Amidst so much beauty it must have been very difficult where to choose.'

'Such was the case. But at last I fixed upon this spot, and have not had reason to regret it.'

'I really must show my wife the delicate curve of this verandah,' said Roberts; and he left Mr. Brade to bring Emily forth.

Roberts found his wife in tears.

'My dear Emily, dry your eyes,' said her husband. 'Here's Brade in an awful rage because that villain watered the wine; but come out and put him in a good humour by praising the verandah, and everything on the premises.'

'And the man said *you* did it, Reginald.'

'What, love?'

'Watered the wine!'

'What a villain!'

'And that's the reason Mr. Brade beat him so unmercifully.'

'Of course, my dear. Brade knows that I'm a gentleman, in every sense of the word – that I'd scorn a low action. He hates a liar, and so do I. He knows *me*, Brade does. Water sherry? No wonder somebody was found to accuse me of forgery! What next? Ah, Emmy dearest, Brade's a man after your husband's own heart.'

'Not in some things, Reginald dear. His manners are too familiar with ladies.'

'Bless your heart, Emmy dear, that's only a way he has. Brade's a gentleman, Emmy, and you may always trust a gentleman – *bred and born*, that is to say. Now, come out and talk to Brade, and make yourself agreeable, while I go and look at his stables. Remember, my own love, that although Brade is kind to me, knowing that I am a gentleman; and although he treats me like an equal, or a superior I may say, knowing, as he does, that I am a first cousin *removed*' – Roberts inwardly laughed when he felt the force of this word – 'to a marchioness, and nephew of the oldest of the Nova Scotia baronets; still, bear in mind that it would be dangerous to both of us if you, by any superciliousness, were to turn his wrath upon *me*.'

'Dear Reginald,' she replied, 'I am too keenly alive to your welfare to admit of my treating unkindly such a friend to you as Mr. Brade appears to be; but I wish George Flower had returned.'

'George Flower! That contemptible constable; that scoundrel that was transported, not for shooting a man, as he says, but for arson, setting fire to a poor farmer's barn. George Flower! My beloved Emily, Brade could crush him whenever he pleased – have him put in irons and sent to Norfolk Island for the remainder of his natural life, the barn-burning convict! George Flower! If I could only tell to you, Emmy, the barbarity of that degraded individual, who, for humanity's sake, I have tolerated out of sheer compassion for the creature, you would shudder, dearest! George Flower! I beg of you, out of respect for me, and the hospitality of my friend Brade, never to mention his name again beneath this aristocratic roof!'

Emily was seldom proof against the eloquence of her husband. Her ideas invariably floated on the rapid stream of words which gushed from his lips, spontaneously; she therefore dried her tears and accompanied Roberts into the verandah, where he left her with Mr. Brade, while he went to the stables, not to look at the horses, but to smoke a pipe and crack coarse jokes with the grooms.

Poor Emily! She was afraid to resent the affront which Mr. Brade's loose discourse afforded her; for he had now given her to understand how completely her convict husband was in his power, and he coupled Roberts and the servant who had recently been thrashed so artfully together that Emily almost fancied she could hear her 'poor Reginald' screaming under a similar affliction.

It was not Mr. Brade's wont to behave unlike a gentleman; but his passions had such an ascendancy over him on that Sunday that he became reckless as to the means by which his purpose could be effected. He had tried soft words without success, and he now adopted *other* measures.

Mr. Brade knew that Emily was a woman of gentle birth and refined education. And he graphically depicted the gulf which yawned between two such beings as herself and her husband. He *asked* Emily how she could have thought of admitting to a place in her affections a person of Roberts's stamp?

Had Mr. Brade been her father, or her brother – and had his object been to dissuade her from *matrimony* – nothing could have been more unexceptionable than was his discourse. But he went on to propose that she should discard the convict, and seek an asylum – a home forever – with him, a man of equal birth, and blood, and rank in life. He offered to resign his appointment and leave the colony with her, and go to any part of the world she thought proper to mention. He told her that an ample fortune would be his on his father's death, and implored her on his knees to listen to his prayers.

Emily hid her face in her hands, and was silent.

Mr. Brade mistook this for an assent, and rising, kissed her several times. She struggled from his embrace, and looked piteously into his eyes; she longed to scream and bring 'Reginald' to her assistance; but alas! She knew the penalty, and, kneeling to Mr. Brade, she prayed to him with clasped hands, and in a subdued voice.

'Spare me, oh, spare me!'

'You are not offended with me?' he inquired.

'No,' she replied, falsely; but her falsehood may be forgiven.

'May I visit you tomorrow?'

'Yes!' (Emily rose, for she heard the voice of her husband, who was now approaching.)

After dinner Mr. Brade tried to make Roberts drunk with wine and flattery. Roberts humoured him, pretended to be speechlessly intoxicated, and snored in an easychair.

Emily endeavoured several times to arouse Roberts; but he acted too well to give her any hope of success. Mr. Brade then bade her contemplate her convict spouse, and criticised him without reserve. And he renewed his offers, his insinuations, and his threats – and, seizing Emily's hand, *kissed* it, to her disgust and horror.

It became late – eleven o'clock – and Emily begged that the horse and gig might be ordered. Mr. Brade assured her that Roberts was not sober enough to drive, and that the road was very dangerous in many places; and he offered to drive her home himself. This Emily declined, and again attempted to arouse her husband.

Mr. Brade retired suddenly from the room. Emily heard him barring the windows and locking the doors at the back part of the house. No time was to be lost! she prudently thought, and slipping from the front door, unobserved, she reached the highroad, bareheaded and unshawled. She did not keep the road, but skirted it, crouching down behind the bushes whenever she fancied she heard footsteps near her. Fortunately it was moonlit, and she was enabled thus to trace her way.

When Mr. Brade had fastened every door and window he returned to the room where he had left Emily. What was his annoyance to find she was gone! He was now alone in the house with Roberts, who pretended still to sleep. Mr. Brade could not believe that Emily had left the villa; he searched every room, looked under every bed, behind every curtain, and into every closet. He then ordered his horse, and galloped along the road, in the hope of overtaking the fugitive.

Emily saw him pass by at full speed, and before she had travelled a mile further, she heard him re-pass, on his return home. Still she kept within the fence until she was out of danger.

It was three o'clock in the morning when Emily, footsore and heartbroken, arrived at her cottage.

CHAPTER XXII

LET THE READER imagine George Flower, with his hair cut as closely as was Roberts's when he came off the treadmill; imagine him unarmed, in the garb of a convict, a dress of coarse yellow and black livery, and a broad arrow painted, or rather tarred, on the yellow parts, to show that he belonged to a road-making gang; a pair of handcuffs on one of his wrists, as though he had succeeded in pulling the left hand through, but could not get the fetter from the right wrist.

Flower soon fell in with that illustrious trio – Millighan, Slobey, and Drohne – who were the terror of the district, and who had recently met the mounted police, and in a fair fight shot two of them, and driven away two others.

'Who are you?' inquired the leader, Millighan.

'A poor devil!' said Flower.

'Why have you these darbys on your right wrist?'

'Because I can't get 'em off.'

'Where have you come from?'

'From a gang about thirty miles from this.'

'Are you a bolter?'

'Yes. They were taking me to get seventy-five*, and I hit

---

* Seventy-five lashes.

the overseer a blow on the head with both hands in the cuffs, and did for him.'

'Did you kill him outright?'

'I should just think I did. I put my foot on his throat and kept it there till he gave over breathing.'

'Then you're a roper*?'

'That same, of course.'

'And a lifer originally?'

'What else? I'm the man that the judge cracked the joke upon.'

'Is transportation for life a joke?'

'No, but when I told him that I committed my crime in "a fit of absence", he said "that's a fit that must last for the remainder of your life!"'

The trio laughed heartily.

'What a jovial judge,' said Millighan, smiling. 'He must have been an Irishman.'

'No, an Englishman,' replied Flower.

'Now, look here, young man,' said Millighan, 'although we think three quite enough, still you are so worthy of being one of us, you shall be added to our number. There is a devilry in your eye, and a taste for fighting about your mouth, that I like amazingly. We're all of us sure to be hanged if we're taken, and therefore you'll have no sort of objection to be shot rather than surrender. We have been out for more than two years, and if we have any luck we will remain the lords of this bush. We are somewhat hard up for flour, and we have come down here on purpose to lighten one of old Captain Piper's drays – I mean the old gentleman who keeps a band, and is fond of dancing. That business concluded, you shall have a comfortable home, and a Tower musket,

---

* A man who is sure to be hanged when apprehended.

and sundry rounds of ball cartridge; and meanwhile here's the horse pistol and the pouch-box which belonged to that unfortunate fellow of the mounted police, who lost his life in a most glorious manner the other day.'

'All right,' said Flower. 'You'll find that I thoroughly understand my business.'

Captain Piper's drays now loomed in the distance.

'Here they come!' cried Millighan. 'And you shall have the honour of speaking first to the drivers.'

The drays, drawn by bullocks, came slowly up the road, and Flower, in a stentorian voice, which charmed the trio, commanded a 'halt'.

The men in charge of the drays instantly surrendered; and Flower, with his usual activity, proceeded to unload the drays of such stores as the trio told him they stood in need of. A bag of English biscuits was found, and the flour therefore remained untouched. Three gallons of French brandy, a small keg of American negrohead tobacco, and a quantity of almonds and raisins were also selected, and a small box containing millinery, silks, ribbons, tapes, bobbins, needles, thread, &c., and – what a prize! – a pair of new double-barrelled pistols, two pairs of plated spurs, a new saddle and bridle, and a small chest filled with various medicines. The drays were then suffered to proceed, and the bushrangers took the shortest road to their habitation.

It was a house made by nature, in a limestone rock, in that region of the world where gold in such quantities is now found. It overlooked a beautiful valley several miles in extent. Cattle were grazing in the valley, and hobbled horses were fattening on the luxuriant pasturage. Pigeons and fowls were feeding about the den, and several large kangaroo dogs barked a welcome to the trio on their return.

There was an old woman in the den, whom the bushrangers called 'Mother', and a girl of about thirteen or fourteen years of age, but prematurely very old looking; this girl they all called 'Sister Sall', but it is doubtful whether she stood in that relationship to any one of them.

On seeing the keg containing the brandy, the old woman was greatly joyed. She speedily produced a large gimlet, pierced the wood, inserted a quill into the aperture, and drew off about a pint, which she fairly distributed amongst the party, including herself and Sister Sall.

Guns, cutlasses, pistols, and powder flasks decorated the walls of the den; and in a corner were several bayonets mounted upon broomsticks, and upon three pegs there were three saddles and bridles, all in excellent condition. Such a collection of miscellaneous articles Flower, even with all his police experience, had never beheld.

The furniture of the den consisted of a table formed of a large piece of limestone, with a flat surface. It had been rolled into the centre of the apartment. The stools were smaller pieces of limestone. On the floor was a Turkey carpet, and upon this the inmates, male and female, used to sleep, covering themselves with blankets, kangaroo skins, and horse rugs, of which there was a superabundance. Millighan, the leader, invariably made a pillow of his saddle.

There was no door to the den; and the fire, around which the dogs congregated by night, was a few paces from the entrance. The den was so dark, even by day, that it was necessary to burn a lamp, but at night it was lighted up with wax or tallow candles.

The old woman made some soup out of the tail of a large kangaroo, and served up an excellent dish composed of boiled macaroni and Westphalia ham. Unexceptionable port wine (lawfully the property of the commandant of Bathurst) was in due course produced. Smoking and drinking then commenced, and in these occupations the old woman and the young girl participated.

George Flower still wore his handcuffs on his wrist. The old woman had steeped his hand in emu oil, and had attempted, but ineffectually, to draw the fetter over the greasy flesh. She now brought a file, and began to cut through the handcuff, and when she grew tired, Sister Sall took up the work. Meanwhile the trio were engaged in playing 'all-fours' with a new pack of cards which had lately come into their possession.

While the old woman was filing his handcuffs, Flower recollected her features. She was a convict who had absconded from the factory at Paramatta, some six years previously, and it was supposed she had perished in the bush. Her name was Elizabeth Norris, but she was more familiarly known to the police authorities as 'Tambourine Bet'. Playing upon the tambourine at fairs was the profession she followed in England before she imbibed a taste for felony, which ended in her being transported for life. The face of the girl was also familiar to Flower, and he racked his brains, but without effect, to bring to recollection whose child she was, and where he had seen her.

'I think that will do,' said Flower, when the process of filing had continued for about two hours; and striking the fetter sharply upon the limestone stool on which he sat, it snapped asunder, and his wrist was once more free.

The trio had finished their game, and were re-filling their pipes and replenishing their tin pannikins with Captain Piper's brandy, when Millighan called out to Flower. 'I say, what's-your-name, give us a song.'

'My name is Teddy Monk,' said Flower.

'Well, then, chant, Monk; and if you can do it as well as you can stop a dray, I make no sort of doubt you'll give universal satisfaction.'

Flower, who was rather proud of his singing, at once indulged the company with a song admirably suited to their tastes. The air of this ditty was that of an Irish jig. It inspirited the old woman, and seizing the instrument from which she derived her cognomen, she cried out, 'Encore', and accompanied Flower with a vigorous beat.

When the song was a second time ended, the old woman got up and danced round the den, as though she were once more on a platform at Greenwich Fair, while Sister Sall, who was by this time intoxicated, clapped her hands, and laughed hysterically. The conviviality was prolonged until the day began to dawn. The inmates of the den then coiled themselves up upon the Turkish carpet which was spread upon the floor, and, one by one, dropped off to sleep.

The only dog which was allowed to come into the den was a small pug-nosed terrier, the property of Millighan. This animal used to sleep at his master's head, his nose resting on the saddle which Millighan used as a pillow.

Flower did not go to sleep. Weary as he was, he lay awake, encompassing the destruction or capture of all the human beings by whom he was surrounded. He raised his head and reconnoitred the den, which was now as still as the grave, while the cocks were crowing, the pigeons cooing, the calves bleating in their pens. He was on the point of getting up stealthily for the purpose of putting his intent into execution, when the terrier growled, and Millighan, awakened, inquired of the dog, 'What's the matter?' The terrier barked; and Flower rejoiced that the dog had no tongue wherewith to answer fully the question that was put to him.

'Hold your noise, you little fool,' said Millighan; but the terrier disobeyed him, and, approaching the spot where Flower lay, recommenced an angry bark, varied occasionally by a surly growl.

'What's the row?' cried Flower, pretending to be awakened.

'Oh! It's only my dog,' replied Millighan. 'He knows you are a stranger, and he can't understand it. Give him a kick, and turn him out of the house.'

'Oh no! He's a good dog,' said Flower. 'What is his name?'

'Nettles,' said Millighan.

'Come here, Nettles; good dog, Nettles,' said Flower, coaxingly.

The dog was not susceptible of flattery. He declined the invitation, and again took up his position near his master's head, where he remained awake, watching, until Flower had fallen asleep.

CHAPTER XXIII

'**M**Y DEAR REGINALD,' said Emily to her husband when he returned from Mr. Brade's, 'why did you take so much wine last night, and compel me to walk home? I could not arouse you, and I could not remain there all night.'

'My beloved,' said Roberts, 'it was very wrong; but remember, it is seldom that one meets a man of one's own cloth. You don't know Brade – you don't know what an actor he is. He has the most intense regard and respect for me, and yet he sometimes, I am told, pretends to run me down behind my back. He does it just to hear what other people say of me. He is a man who is full of fun.'

'Fun, Reginald?'

'Yes, my love, pure fun, I assure you. Don't offend Brade, whatever you do. He has pledged me his word that I shall have a free pardon immediately, and for my sake do not make an enemy of a man who can be, if he likes, such a valuable friend. He is coming to dine here tomorrow quietly, and hear you sing and play. I told him we should make no preparation for him; but you must see that there is a particularly nice dinner put upon the table, and I will order in some excellent wine and a very *recherché* dessert.'

'I am not equal to entertaining Mr. Brade, Reginald,' replied Emily. 'The dinner shall be provided, but I will not appear.'

'Emily, my love, you really must make an effort on this occasion,' said Roberts. 'Remember, dearest, for my sake, for the sake of my emancipation from this loathsome place of bondage, it is your duty to conciliate Brade, and not repulse him.'

Emily, who had not the faintest idea of the real character of the man to whom she was linked, was afraid to mention to him all that had passed on the previous day. She therefore gave as a reason for her disinclination to appear at the dinner that she was poorly and out of spirits.

'But you will be better by tomorrow, my own dearest Emmy. My life, my soul, you know what sacrifices your Reginald is prepared to make for *you*, and he knows she will not disappoint him in this, will she, my own dear pet?' and Roberts, placing his arm around Emily's neck, gently patted her cheek, and looked tenderly into her soft hazel eyes, which were filling with tears.

With an aching heart, Emily promised that she would appear at the dinner table on the following day, and that she would do her utmost to delight with music and her voice the gentleman who seemed to take advantage of her husband's position, and who, under the impunity which that position afforded him, was resolved to persist in his infamous pursuit.

~

Roberts had of late frequently absented himself from the office in which he was employed, and spent his stolen leisure at a cottage where resided a young lady who had recently attracted his attention. This was no other than one of Emily's fellow passengers, whose conduct on the voyage has been already described. It amused Roberts vastly to hear of Emily's 'greenness' from the lips of this person, who used to accompany her details with mimicry. Thus entertained, Roberts would lie on the sofa, smoke his cigar, and drink Madeira, on those days when he felt indisposed for work.

Mr. Brade knew of this, and, a few days after he had dined at the cottage, called one morning, and delicately conveyed to Mrs. Harcourt 'what a pity, what a shame it was, that a man who was so blest with a beautiful and accomplished woman for his wife, should be so lost to every sense of propriety as to indulge in such disreputable company'.

Mr. Brade's motive was obvious, and Emily saw that he wished to estrange her affections from her husband. She therefore concluded that Mr. Brade's story was an invention. The idea of Reginald being unfaithful! It was absurd.

Had she been in other circumstances, Emily would have said this aloud, and ordered Mr. Brade to leave her house, and never more enter it; but as it was, she was compelled to remain silent, and listen to offers which Mr. Brade never failed to repeat whenever he had an opportunity.

Although Mr. Brade's story was not credited by Emily, nevertheless it added to her miseries. The bare thought of 'Reginald' taking a delight in the society of any other woman distracted her.

'Reginald,' said Emily, one night, 'I have such awful dreams, I am afraid to go to bed. I dream that you love someone else.'

'My darling!' exclaimed Roberts, 'is it not proverbial that ridiculous fancies, the most improbable things, present themselves to our imagination when we are asleep? You *dream* that I could be so wicked? May you continue so to dream, dearest. Oh, Emmy! Why do you torture me? No, never, my love!'

CHAPTER XXIV

THERE WERE TO be races at Paramatta, fifteen miles from Sydney. Roberts asked Emily if she would like to visit them. He knew full well that she would decline. Roberts, therefore, left his house alone, in his gig, drawn by his fine-actioned, fast-stepping trotting horse, one of the best animals in the colony.

Roberts drove to the top of Church-Hill, and there took up the Enchantress (he so called his new acquaintance), who was dressed in pink silk, trimmed with black lace, and wore a veil of white lace upon a white straw bonnet, and carried a beautiful parasol, fringed with blue floss silk.

Roberts's turnout was the neatest of its kind on the crowded road; and his famous horse, *Bosphorus*, suffered nothing to pass him. In the boot of the gig was a small ham, a pair of cold fowls, several French rolls, and half a dozen bottles of champagne.

Mr. Brade knew that Roberts was going to the races in the young lady's company, and he determined to 'satisfy' Emily, beyond a doubt, that Reginald was not what she took him to be. Mr. Brade, therefore, ordered one of his constables to proceed to the races, and carry out certain instructions.

It was a lovely day. Everybody in the colony appeared to have congregated on the Paramatta racecourse.

Roberts had 'shown off' his magnificent trotter, his light gig, and silver plated harness, to the admiring spectators; had lost a dozen pair of gloves to the Enchantress, by giving her the field against the favourite; and it was now time for them to discuss the delicacies in the boot of the gig.

When in the very act of carving the ham, having given his companion the liver wing of one of the fowls, the constable approached Roberts and said, 'Please may I ask who you are, sir?'

'I am Mr. Roberts.'

'Well, but, Mr. Roberts, what I wish to know is, are you free or bond?'

'Why, free; free as air, or a bird on the ocean wave.'

'Now, I don't want to take any undue advantage of you,' said the constable, 'and I therefore repeat the question, are you a free man, or are you a prisoner of the Crown?'

'Have some ham and fowl, and a glass of champagne?'

'Put down that knife and fork, and answer my questions. Are you a free man?'

'Not exactly.'

'Are you an assigned servant? Or are you in the service of Government?'

'Assigned.'

'To whom?'

'To my wife.'

'Is this lady your wife?'

'No; she's a friend of my wife.'

'Is your wife on the racecourse?'

'No, she's in Sydney.'

'Will you oblige me with a sight of your pass?'

'Pass! My good sir! Do you suppose it necessary for me to carry a pass?'

'You haven't a pass?'

'No.'

'Then I am sorry to say I am compelled to take you into custody for being an assigned servant 'at large', without a pass from his mistress; and as a convict cannot possess property, I am bound to believe that everything about you belongs to your mistress; so, pack up and come along with me. And you, madam, must go too, for how do I know that all that finery you've got on isn't the property of the lady to whom this man belongs?'

Roberts's companion instantly discharged a volley of abuse at the constable, but this had the effect of making him even more disagreeable.

Roberts took out his purse, and offered it to the constable. The constable put it into his pocket, then searched Roberts, and took from his person a penknife, a pencil case, and a tollbar ticket. He also took Roberts's gold watch and chain, and the ruby pin which fastened his blue satin scarf. This operation was performed amidst the laughter and jeers of the multitude, who had now formed a ring round Roberts's horse and gig.

Roberts was then handcuffed, and a small rope tied to the handcuffs, and fastened to one of the springs of his vehicle. The constable then got into the gig, and, sitting beside the Enchantress, triumphantly drove off the course, with Roberts in tow, cheered by the mob, who seemingly enjoyed the joke – for Roberts had attracted considerable notice upon the road.

Proceeding, as this interesting *cortège* did, at an easy pace, it was passed by all those who were returning from the races; and the majority of the company now labouring under the excitement which is caused by frequent drams, the quantity of personal pleasantry which was scattered upon Roberts and the Enchantress was enormous.

When they were within about five miles of Sydney, there came on one of those violent storms of wind called, in the colony of New South Wales, 'a brickfielder'. This covered everyone with red dust, and the wind being followed almost immediately by a heavy fall of rain, anything more grotesque than became the plight of the party it would be difficult to conceive. Roberts, who was greatly fatigued, was continually imploring the constable not to let the horse walk so fast, a request which was commonly responded to in the words, 'Hold your tongue, and don't disturb us', for the woman had now made herself more agreeable to the constable than, under the circumstances, he had any right to expect.

They were now at the door of Emily's cottage. Mr. Brade was in the cottage at the time. He had been there for at least two hours, apologising in the most abject tone for any levity of demeanour of which in previous interviews he had been guilty.

'Dear me! What's this?' cried Mr. Brade, looking out of the window. 'Dear me! No! It can't be. Yes, it is. Let me conceal myself. If the constable sees me here, I'm ruined. What crime can he have committed? He may be brought up before me! Pray, Mrs. Harcourt, let me conceal myself. Look out of the window!' Mr. Brade rushed into the next room, and almost fainted with the convulsive laughter into which that magnificent spectacle had thrown him.

Emily immediately recognised the creature who had so often chilled her blood on the passage to New South Wales. She did not at first see Reginald. What a constable and this horrid woman could be doing in Reginald's gig at her door was more than Emily could comprehend.

The constable came in and detailed all that had taken place, leaving Reginald and his companion still outside, the latter seated in the gig holding the reins, and the former in handcuffs tied to the tail of the vehicle.

Emily was stupefied, but believing Reginald to have been a victim of conspiracy in the matter which originally brought him to the colony, she was not prepared to condemn him until she had heard what he had to say in his defence. She therefore told the constable that Roberts was at the races with her consent, and desired that he might be immediately set at liberty.

'And what about the lady, mam?' said the constable. 'May I take her home in the gig, mam? Poor thing, she is very wet.'

'You must use your own discretion in that matter; speak to my husband,' said Emily.

The constable *did* use his own discretion, and very humanely drove the Enchantress to her abode, where he received at her hands a bottle of brandy for his trouble.

Roberts threw himself upon the couch in his dining-room, and stretched himself at full length. He was too tired to pull off his wet clothes and boots.

'Dearest,' he gasped, 'a spoonful – a spoonful, Emmy, dearest, of brandy – I'm regularly dead beat!'

Mr. Brade was looking through the keyhole, and was longing to laugh at Roberts's miserable but well-merited condition; but when he beheld Emily administering to his wants, and holding up his head, while he drank the liquor from her hand, his soul was consumed by a variety of passions which were never before perhaps blended simultaneously in the same bosom. Love, pity, envy, hate, jealousy, anger, joy, and sorrow were all at work together, and Mr. Brade said within his heart, 'That man or I must leave this colony, if not this world.'

'Flower! That villain Flower! Oh, the scoundrel!' groaned Roberts. 'He promised that he would show me that the transfer of myself to you would not better my condition. Who but Flower would have thus insulted me? I could have borne all but being mixed up with that horrible woman. Oh, Emmy, judge of what my feelings have been!'

Roberts was sincere in his belief that George Flower was the author of his misfortune, and the conjecture did credit to his sagacity, for it was just the trick Flower would have played him, only that he would not have allowed Emily to see the young lady.

A light was now breaking in upon Emily. She began to see through it all (she thought). 'Poor Reggie! Let me take off these wet boots and change your clothes, dear; and then tell me all that has happened.' In a whisper she added, 'Mr. Brade is in the next room. He ran in there to escape being seen by the constable.'

'Oh, Mr. Brade is here! I am glad of that,' said Roberts. 'For he will *see* how I have been treated, and will have justice done to me. Oh, Emmy! I have not a leg to stand on.'

When Roberts had attired himself in dry clothes, Mr. Brade made his appearance, and heard the complaint preferred against the constable. A more plausible story was never uttered. Roberts had hatched it on the road, and in point of 'circumstantiality' it was perfect.

He had left his gig (he said), and had gone into the race-stand. When he returned he found that abominable female seated in the vehicle – polluting the very harness upon the back of the horse. He requested her in the most polite manner to leave his gig immediately. She abused him, and called him all sorts of names.

Emily here said she could believe it. *She* had heard the creature in a passion.

'Well,' continued Roberts, 'what could I do? I was obliged to call a constable to take her in charge. The constable came. He happened to be a friend of the woman. "Give me in charge!" said the woman. "Who are you? What are you? You are a convict. Give me in charge? I give you in charge for assaulting me!" The constable took her part, and then took me into custody. And, to show the animus of the man, he drove her to town in the gig, and tied me, handcuffed, behind, as you saw with your own eyes, Emmy, dearest.'

Emily had seen it, of course; and what was more, the constable had had the audacity to speak kindly of the woman, and pity her, and then take her away in Reginald's gig; and she saw the man laughing when he left the house! Emily was, therefore, perfectly satisfied that Reginald had been most grossly ill-treated; but she did not as yet perceive how George Flower was a party to this infamous proceeding.

Roberts explained. Flower was a friend of this constable, who acknowledged that he had promised Flower to keep an eye on him.

Mr. Brade, who felt that Roberts's cunning had completely baffled his project, pretended to be very angry with the constable.

'I cannot advise you,' said Mr. Brade, 'to press the charge in public; but I will see that both that man and George Flower are dismissed from the police.'

CHAPTER XXV

MILLIGHAN AND HIS gang never left the precincts of the den except they were in want of supplies; and being now provided with all they required for the present, they engaged in the many pastimes within their reach. Shooting and kangarooing during the day – cards, tobacco, and grog at night. Flower rather enjoyed the life, and had grown to like the captain of the gang. In addition to being a very plucky fellow, Millighan rode well and swam well, was a good shot both with gun and pistol; could tell a pleasant story, sing sentimental songs, and was an ardent admirer of the fair sex. In short, he was very like George Flower in disposition and accomplishments – as good looking, and as active.

Millighan, in turn, had conceived a great regard for Flower, and had said to George, one day, when they were out kangarooing on horseback, 'If I should get knocked over in the next battle we have with the mounted police, you are the man to stand in my shoes.' Ay, and Millighan had endeared himself to Flower by other means. He had, unconsciously, aroused George's pride and tickled his vanity: and to this he was indebted for his life; for Flower's opportunities of destroying him were now frequent. Millighan had one night (little conscious in whose presence he was speaking) held forth on the nobleness of Flower's character.

'He is not one of your chicken-hearted dogs that fire at a man from behind a tree,' said Millighan. 'He never employs those black beasts to track up his prey. He goes out into the open, like a man, and challenges his adversary. If I had been in that gang, when Flower was shot in the back on the Liverpool Road, I'd have killed the cowardly villain who did such a thing. It's a great pity that Flower did not take to the bush instead of the police. He would have gone down to posterity in the annals of this blessed country, in the absence of patriots, as one of her greatest men.'

~

It was now time for another visit to the roads. The tea and sugar were exhausted, and there was but very little tobacco remaining.

Slobey was left at home to assist the old woman in the den.

Millighan, Drohne, and Flower, each armed with a carbine and a pair of horse pistols, descended the hill on which their limestone house was situated. They were on this occasion on horseback, and were, moreover, dressed in the uniform and appointments of the men of the mounted police, and they wore their regulation broadswords, and the horses they rode were the property of Government.

After winding five miles, over crags and creeks, and through valleys and forests, the bushrangers reached the high road, of which for the past two years they had been the terror.

'Monk,' said Millighan to Flower, 'have you a mind for a lark?'

'Yes,' responded George. 'I'm up to anything. What is it to be?'

'Why, look here. Let us pay a visit to old Grimes, and taste of his hospitality. He is very fond of entertaining the mounted police, and lending them stores when they run short. And he may give us a newspaper or two.'

'But does he not know the men of the mounted police?' inquired Flower.

'Not all of 'em. How should he?' returned Millighan. 'Thanks to the accuracy of my eye, they are changed pretty often in these parts.'

Major Grimes had been a major in the Royal Artillery. He was now a settler, possessed of large flocks of sheep, near Bathurst. His store houses were usually well filled with supplies of all kinds, and it was quite true that he had been very accommodating to the men of the mounted corps, whom he was always glad to see upon his premises.

The bushrangers rode on, and at length arrived at Major Grimes's estate, where they were welcomed warmly, invited to alight, and take some refreshment in the kitchen. Had the Major any news? Yes, the body, or rather, the remains of a body, had been found in the Hawkesbury River, and had been identified as those of the famous thief-taker George Flower! It was supposed he had been murdered; though one paper hinted, that, as he was drunk when last seen upon the road, it was not improbable that he met his death by attempting to swim across.

All expressed their great regret at this; and Flower had again the satisfaction of hearing his own praises sounded by Millighan. He joined in those praises, and was very eloquent on his own bravery – though he expressed a decided opinion that George Flower was a great vagabond, and too grasping after rewards for the apprehension of desperate characters.

'Talking of desperate characters,' said Millighan to the Major, 'what think you of that unfortunate affair in which some of our fellows were engaged, and two killed?'

'Yes, it was a sad business,' replied the Major, 'but what could you do – four against nine? Such awful odds.'

'Awful!' said Millighan. 'And all nine brave men, too.'

'And daring,' added the Major.

'Yes, and daring,' conceded Millighan. 'But we shall have better luck soon, I hope.'

'I hope so, too,' said the Major, 'for I have several drays on the road, about which I am beginning to be very nervous. They took everything from Captain Piper's drays a short time ago.'

'So I hear,' said Millighan, 'but I don't believe a word of it. If these drivers are stopped at all, and robbed of only a few articles, they sell the rest, and go home empty. At least, that's my opinion, Major. Of course, I may be wrong.'

'Here's a nice slander upon your cloth, Corporal, in the last *Australian*,' said the Major.

'What's that, sir?'

'Why, they say that the mounted police sometimes doff their clothes, hide their horses, put on smock frocks and hairy caps – and help themselves to people's property.'

Millighan and his companions laughed the idea to scorn, and appealed to each other as to the possibility of such a thing.

'If the mounted police want anything, they have only to ask for it,' said Millighan. 'At this present we are out of tea, sugar, tobacco, and spirits, and if you could supply us with some, for the price of which I will give you an order on Lieutenant Mole, our commanding officer, in Bathurst Town, we shall be very much obliged to you.'

'Oh, certainly! How much do you require?' asked the Major.

'Why, sir, about five pounds of tea, fifteen pounds of sugar, three pounds of tobacco, and about a gallon of rum, gin, or brandy,' said Millighan.

While these stores were being weighed out, Millighan wrote an order for payment on Lieutenant Mole, and signed it – 'Walker, lance corporal.'

'Corporal, will you allow me to speak a few words to you in private?' said Major Grimes.

'By all means, sir,' said Millighan, following the Major into the verandah, where he walked up and down – his heavy sabre in its steel scabbard dangling at his side.

'Corporal,' said Major Grimes, confidentially, 'a shepherd of mine this morning told me that he knows the very spot which those desperate dogs make their headquarters.'

'Indeed!' said Millighan. 'And where may the spot be?'

'That's the point,' said the Major. 'The fellow knows the secret is worth something, and he won't tell; but he says he'll point it out if we will go with him and take a large force, and promise to obtain for him a pardon, and give him a portion of the reward that is offered: three of their number are worth £300 – a hundred each, you know.'

'The man's terms are very moderate,' said Millighan, 'very moderate. Of his free pardon he would he quite sure; but if he wants a good share of the money, the fewer that have to do with the capture the better. Let me and my men have some conversation with him, and who knows that by this time tomorrow we may not have the whole gang, dead or alive?'

Flower was now summoned to the council. He heard with well-acted delight what the Major communicated, entirely agreed with Millighan that the fewer who had a hand in the capture the better, and proposed that the shepherd should be at once sent for and questioned.

The shepherd repeated his story – that he had seen the den at a distance, and could point it out, for he had marked with a tomahawk several leading trees as landmarks; but he said he could not *describe* the way to the den, it was so intricate and roundabout. From his description of the den, there could be no doubt that he *was* possessed of the secret, which, as Major Grimes had truly observed, was well worth knowing.

At first the shepherd declined to go, unless accompanied by a large force; but after a while he yielded to the persuasive arguments of Millighan, which Flower was compelled to support.

'How did you happen to stumble across it, my man?' inquired Millighan, when they were about two miles distant from the road, and in the heart of a forest peopled only by kangaroos, opossums, and wild cats.

'Why, one day,' the shepherd replied, 'I was out looking for a working bullock in this direction, and I lost my way, and had to sleep in the bush all night. Next morning, when daylight appeared, I wandered about, almost starved to death, when suddenly I came upon the print of a horse's foot. This I followed, and at last came upon a path, where I came upon the print of a *dog's* foot, which was quite fresh. "Hulloa," says I, "I can't be far off some cattle station," and I followed the track for about three mile, when I came to a creek, where I saw a horse drinking. Now that horse belonged to a gentleman who had it stole. It belonged to one of Billy Wentworth's overseers, and there was the w.c.w. branded on the shoulder, plain enough. Oh, oh, thought I, the sooner I go back the better, for, mind you, these fellows make pretty short work of anybody who happens to get a scent of where they are: they think nothing of tying a fellow to a tree and leaving him there till his skeleton is discovered.'

'Nonsense!' cried Drohne, who had twice performed this cruel operation, when the gang was short of powder, and could not afford to throw away a single charge in destroying an enemy; for every man who knew of the den's whereabouts could be regarded in no other light.

'Well, go on,' said Millighan.

'Well, while I was looking at the horse, and thinking that I'd make the best of my way back, I saw smoke about a hundred yards off, and heard the barking of dogs——'

Drohne cocked his carbine, took it from the socket, and looked fiercely at the shepherd; but Millighan frowned at his comrade, and checked his impetuosity.

'Just as I was going away I saw three men coming along. I was in an awful fright, and crouched down behind a big piece of stone, and they passed without seeing me.'

'Should you know them again?' asked Drohne, once more placing his hand on his carbine.

'Oh, yes,' said the shepherd. 'They were drest in jackets and caps made out of the skins of flying squirrels, and were talking about a robbery they had committed only a few days before. But we had better talk quietly now, for we are not far from the creek, where I saw the horse. As I live, there he is, lame as a cat in the fore shoulder.'

'Who's to do it?' shouted Drohne to Millighan.

'Hold your tongue!' said Millighan, in reply.

'What are you about?' screamed Flower to Drohne, who was now taking aim at the shepherd's head. 'Hold hard! If you pull that trigger, I'll send a ball into you.'

The shepherd was rather bewildered. He fancied that Drohne wanted to shoot him, in order to prevent his receiving any share of the reward; and he addressed himself to the whole party touching the unfairness of such a deed.

'Answer me one question,' said Millighan. 'Is there anyone else who knows the road to this den?'

'Not a soul,' was the reply.

'Did you mention it to no-one?'

'No, I was not such a fool. I told master that I knew where the den was, but I would not tell him even the direction it was in. But let us not make a noise, for look, there's the smoke! And don't you hear the dogs bark? You go on, and I'll wait here. Give me something or other to defend myself with, for they'll be sure to show fight.'

Drohne was still disposed to shoot the shepherd, and could not understand on what principle Millighan and Flower objected.

'Come along,' said Millighan to the man. 'You'll find there will be no fighting.'

What was the shepherd's astonishment to find that the dogs recognised this curious branch of the police, and frisked around their horses in an agony of delight at their approach. The shepherd's want of comprehension on this head, however, was soon supplied, when he found himself in irons.

CHAPTER XXVI

I N CONSEQUENCE OF the scene which had taken place upon the racecourse, Roberts lost his employ in the attorney's office, and Emily's pupils were all withdrawn from her. Parents were unwilling that their children should come into contact with a person who had such a husband. In order, therefore, to earn daily bread, Emily was compelled to do needlework, and knit socks and comforters.

The *Lady Jane Grey* paid another visit to Sydney, and old Captain Dent lost no time in finding Emily, who was still living in the cottage he had taken for her. Emily was delighted to see the old man, the more especially as he had come at the very moment when she most needed a protector, for Mr. Brade had thrown out a dark hint that he intended to have Roberts taken away from her, and assigned to himself.

Captain Dent used to visit Emily very often, and his presence bored Mr. Brade beyond measure. To Mr. Brade's horror the old man used to invite Emily to return to England with him, offering her a stern cabin and a free passage.

One day Mr. Brade sent for Roberts, and said to him, 'Do you know, that vulgar old ship captain is far too intimate with your wife?'

Roberts, quite unmoved, notwithstanding the grave character of the suspicion, replied that it might be so, and a legal idea suddenly flashed across his mind. The idea was this, whether a convict assigned to his wife could bring an action for criminal conversation? Whether being attainted by felony destroyed certain rights or not? Of his wife's innocence he had no sort of doubt, but that was not his 'point'. His point was to get money out of Captain Dent's pocket, and Captain Dent out of Mr. Brade's way. This was what Roberts called 'a very comprehensive move'.

Emily had shown to her husband all the letters the Captain had recently written to her. They were conceived and expressed in a tone of the most affectionate regard.

Captain Dent had frequently been shut up in the same room alone with Emily for hours, and half-a-dozen little circumstances might be brought forward, which, if put together, would be ample to satisfy the law. 'But then, again,' – it was thus Roberts argued – 'this would be cutting up the goose for the golden egg, for Emmy would leave me and go home, and I might fall into the hands of some master who would make me work, and bring me perhaps before Brade for idleness, and Brade would order me fifty lashes as soon as look at me, if Emmy was once out of the colony.' So Roberts abandoned the project which at first had appeared to him so glittering. But, in so much as he would not be safe if he were indifferent to Mr. Brade's wishes, he spoke to his wife on the subject, and requested her in future not to be at home when Captain Dent called.

It was a great sacrifice to Emily to forego the pleasure of receiving the old man who had treated her with such uniform kindness; but slave as she was to the wishes of her husband, she consented without a murmur, albeit she laughed at the very idea that 'Reginald' could think of being jealous of an old gentleman whose age was more than double that of herself, while he did not appear at all jealous of Mr. Brade, whose visits were quite as frequent as those of Captain Dent, and whose attentions were much more marked, even in 'Reginald's' presence.

CHAPTER XXVII

FLOWER WAS FAR from weary of the wild marauding life that he was leading, but he had a curious dream on the night which introduced Major Grimes's shepherd to the den, and he made up his mind to bring matters to a speedy conclusion, so far as related to the capture of the gang. He asked Millighan to walk with him to the top of a mountain, which overlooked the den, and there he discoursed with Millighan for some time on the grandeur of the scene, and the sweets of liberty. It was a beautiful warm day, and not a cloud to be seen in the sky. The foot of man had never before trod the ground on which Flower and Millighan were then standing. The stillness amidst the huge rocks of limestone conveyed an idea of something awful. The place was uninhabited, even by the birds of the air or the beasts of the field.

'Millighan,' said Flower, resting his arms across the muzzle of his carbine, and peering into Millighan's eyes, 'could you commit murder?'

'Not in cold blood,' said Millighan. 'Why do you ask me that question?'

'Because I wish to know your sentiments on that head,' said Flower. 'I could shoot a man, or be shot at, Millighan, without a flinch, but I could not kill a brave fellow from behind a tree, or take a dirty advantage of a living creature worthy of the name of man.'

'Well, that's what *I* feel,' said Millighan.

'Now, look here,' said Flower. 'Suppose a mounted policeman, or a thief-taker – a fellow of real pluck – was to come upon you when you were alone, and challenge you to surrender, what would you do? Would you draw your trigger at once, and not give him a chance?'

'No!' cried Millighan. 'I'd tell him to stand off and have a fight for it.'

'Millighan,' said Flower, still keeping his eagle eye firmly fixed on Millighan's, 'are you speaking the truth?'

'Yes, so help me heaven!'

'Now let us suppose that such a man as that fellow George Flower – the fellow who was drowned the other day – was to be in the same position with you as I am now?'

'I'd tell him,' said Millighan, 'that one of us must die, and challenge him to fight fair!'

'How fight fair?'

'Why, I'd ask him to measure off fifty yards – to walk backwards five and twenty paces, and let me do the like.'

'And do you think he would agree?'

'Yes, I do; for he was a man. I have often longed to meet that fellow in the field, for what I most love in this life is its excitement, and to be killed by the hand of a man like Flower, or to escape by killing him, in fair fight – either way, it would be something to suit me.'

'Millighan,' said Flower, 'I believe every word that you have uttered. Now, listen to what I am going to tell you. I *am* George Flower!'

Millighan started, and stared at Flower, whose eyes were now riveted on those of his adversary.

Millighan's carbine dropped from his hand, but he did not change colour, or betray any alarm.

'Pick up your piece,' said Flower, pointing to the carbine, and assuming a proud but careless attitude. 'I am all that you have said of me, Millighan. I might have shot you like a dog before I spoke to you just now; but I could not do that, for you are a man, as well as myself, and you are as brave and as generous. Pick up your piece, and walk backwards five and twenty paces. But let us shake hands first.'

Millighan took Flower's hand, and sighed heavily.

'Don't surrender,' suggested Flower, half fearing that Millighan would do so, and break the very charm that bound him to the man.

'Surrender!' cried Millighan, with a smile and a sneer. 'No, I'll never do that. And knowing you to be a brave foe, I have still a chance. But tell me, are you in earnest? Are you really George Flower? Yes, you must be. And hear this' – his blood began to warm – 'if you are *not*, we must fight this day, for we cannot after this live together.'

Millighan took up his carbine, satisfied himself that there was powder in the pan, and with his left thumb pushed the corner of the flint round, so as to insure ignition when he drew the trigger.

Flower placed his carbine against a huge stone, put his hands into his pockets, and looked firmly at Millighan: 'I *am* George Flower!' said he. 'Who but George Flower would deal with you as I do? Don't let us talk much, or I may forget my mission, and become a bushranger myself.'

Flower then took up his carbine, examined the powder in the pan, and touched the flint, as Millighan had done.

'Flower! For Flower you must be,' said Millighan, 'grant me, if you shoot me, one desire that I have had from boyhood – a desire that has haunted me. I do not dread death, but I have a horror of burial. If I fall, suffer me to lie on the very spot. Let the eagle come and feast upon my carcass, pluck these eyes from their sockets, and the skin from this brow. Let me lie here in this lonely region, and let my bones bleach in the sun, and the rain fall, and the moon and the stars shine upon them.'

'My God!' exclaimed Flower, seizing Millighan by the arm. 'The same dread of being buried has ever haunted *me*. If *I* fall by your hand, let me rest here, with my head pillowed upon this gun. Let no man living be shown the spot where I fell.'

'Take your ground,' said Millighan. 'I am ready.'

'There is my hand,' said Flower. 'And should we meet in another world we shall not be ashamed of one another.'

Tears were starting in the eyes of both Flower and Millighan. Each stepped backward pace for pace, Millighan followed by the little terrier, Nettles. When they were about fifty yards apart they halted and looked at each other for several moments. Both simultaneously levelled their carbines, but each was indisposed to be the first to fire. Millighan discharged his piece. He had aimed at Flower's heart. His bullet whizzed past Flower's head, and carried away a part of the left whisker.

Flower fired – and Millighan fell flat on his face! The ball had entered his left breast. Flower ran to the spot, to catch any last word Millighan might desire to breathe – but——

Millighan was dead!

The dog Nettles became frantic. He flew at Flower, bit him in the legs, and stood over his late master, barking defiantly. Flower could not drive the dog away without violence, which he would not resort to, and he could not, therefore, even touch the bushranger's corpse, now weltering in its blood.

Millighan's gun was still grasped in his lifeless hand, and there Flower suffered it to remain.

'That head,' muttered Flower to himself, while the tears streamed down his cheeks, 'is worth a hundred pounds; but I could not cut it off for a hundred thousand, and *fifty* free pardons.'

'Nettles, come!' said Flower to the dog. 'I'll take care of you, Nettles.' But the terrier only growled in reply, and took up a position near his late master's head, and there remained.

~

The capture of the other two bushrangers was as easy as possible to a man of Flower's strength of mind and body. On returning to the den, he found only the shepherd, who was still in irons, and the two women. Drohne and Slobey had gone out kangarooing.

Flower released the shepherd, gave him a double-barrelled gun, and told him to use it, if he were ordered to do so.

Bet and Sal were handcuffed together, and placed in an aperture of the den; Flower and the shepherd then awaited the return of Drohne and Slobey.

Flower had been remarkably abstemious of late. His sagacity had pointed out to him that if he drank too much he might talk too much, and be led into boasting, which would be dangerous. But now that Millighan was no more, and the arrangements for his comrades' capture quite complete, he went into 'the spirit-room', and drank four drams. 'Here's to the memory of that brave man!' said Flower, drinking the first dram at a gulp. 'And here's to my noble self! And here's to that dear woman, Mr. Orford's daughter! And here's to the girls that love George Flower!'

Flower's tongue, too, had been tied up of late. He had not been able to 'hold forth' in the strain he was accustomed to indulge in; and such a volume of words and phrases pent up for so many weeks was almost the death of him. He was dying to abuse somebody, and lacked the provocation until Drohne and Slobey appeared; for Flower could not address any unkind discourse to the women; on the contrary, when he was handcuffing them and putting them away, he said, in the most gentle and earnest manner imaginable, 'My sweet dears, it's only a matter of form, which must be gone through, for safety's sake.'

Of handcuffs there was an abundance in the den, and Flower began to manipulate the assortment, and select such as would best fit Drohne and Slobey.

'Now, then, shepherd,' said Flower, 'when these two gentlemen arrive, you will be so good as to put these things round their wrists. So, do you see? I'll cover them with this double-barrelled gun; do you see? This is the way to handcuff two men together – so, do you see? Hands across, down the middle.'

These instructions had scarcely been given, when Flower heard voices outside the den.

'Here they come!' said Flower. 'Now for it!'

Drohne and Slobey were unarmed.

'Don't get off your horses!' cried Flower, levelling his gun at Drohne.

'Why not?' said Drohne and Slobey.

'Because you are my prisoners; and if you don't do as I tell you, I'll drop you right and left, just as I would quail.'

'What lark are you up to?' asked Drohne.

'You will see that presently,' said Flower. 'Ride close together; do you hear? There! That'll do. Now, then, my gentle shepherd, receive their wrists prettily. Not that way, stupid. Hands across, didn't I tell you? There! Thank you, shepherd; that will do. Now, then, bring out another pair or two of handcuffs.'

(The handcuffs were brought.)

'Hold this gun, shepherd, and shoot the first man who moves his hand against me,' said Flower.

'What is all this, Teddy? Where's Millighan? Have you been drinking, and gone mad?' inquired Drohne.

'What an impatient fellow you are!' exclaimed Flower. 'Wait a bit, and you will see through it all.'

Here Flower handcuffed together a stirrup iron of either saddle, so that the *horses* were coupled. The reins of the bridles were then drawn over the heads of the horses and given to the shepherd to hold.

The women were now released, and ordered to bring up four of the other horses (government cattle), then grazing in the valley. While they were absent, Flower, unseen, possessed himself of all the gold and jewellery in the den, and packed it carefully in two new saddle-bags. 'This is for Gov'ment,' he remarked to himself, with a wink which denied the truth of his statement in this particular. 'Why, this bus'ness, one way or other, will be worth about eight hundred pound to me,' he added, filling his pipe, and looking searchingly round the den. 'I shall get bounty money on all these horses, and saddles, and guns, and such like; and then these two are worth a hundred a piece, and Bet ought to be worth something, as she has been a bolter at large for upwards of four years. Gov'ment's very liberal, I must say, in some things, though stingy in others. Poor Millighan! He very nearly did it for me. How that ball whistled!' Here Flower smiled, and scratched that part of his jaw which Millighan's bullet had shorn of its whisker. He then went outside and used some very arrogant language to his prisoners, who could not *yet* understand him thoroughly.

The women had now returned with the horses.

'Saddle 'em, my gals,' said Flower. 'Saddle 'em, and tonight we'll drink with old Grimes, and perhaps kiss that pretty girl in the kitchen. Oh dear! It's a fairy world after all. Saddle the nags, my gals. Help 'em, shepherd. I'll hold these gentlemen's horses.'

Flower took the reins, and stroked the noses of the steeds on which his prisoners sat.

The horses were saddled.

'Now, then, shepherd, take the reins of these gentlemen's horses once more, while I go inside with Bet and Sal.'

These orders were obeyed, and Flower and the females retired to the den.

'Dress yourselves in the gorgeous array of the mounted police,' said Flower.

Bet urged that it would be impossible for *her* to do this; but Flower insisted on the difficulty being overcome.

'Of *course*, put on the boots and spurs, and pouch-belt, and all the rest of it,' said Flower, in reply to a question from the woman. 'And now you, Sally, come you here, and let Bet dress you up in proper character. What a noble face you have for a private! Come along!'

The girl appeared to enter into the joke, and obeyed the mandate with alacrity.

'Now then, Bet, bring something to drink upon the road,' said Flower, 'for it's a precious long ride, and we shall all be dry before we reach old Grimes's.'

Bet provided herself with a bottle of brandy, and Sal put a tin pannikin into the bosom of the uniform jacket, which was much too large for her.

The only armed person of the party was George Flower. He carried a carbine, a pair of loaded pistols, and a sword.

'Shepherd, mount your horse, and lead the way!' cried Flower. 'And you, gentlemen, ride behind him, as you now are. You get up, Bet, and ride on my right; and you, Sal, come to the left. Now, then, look alive!'

'What about the dogs?' inquired the woman.

'Oh, they may come with us,' said Flower; 'the whole lot of 'em. Call to them.'

The dogs, some seven in number, were called; they came, and the party, or rather the procession, moved on.

Bet complained of being tired when she had ridden about nine miles; but Flower drank with her, and cheered for awhile her flagging spirits. He then recommended her to have a race with Sal for a quarter of a mile; but she had no ambition to shine in equestrian performances, and began to abuse Flower with matchless volubility, without producing, however, any effect, beyond that of making him laugh immoderately.

Suddenly Drohne pulled up his horse, and Slobey was obliged to do the like.

'What's the row?' Flower inquired.

'The row is this,' said Drohne. 'I'll go no further with you, you hang-dog fiend.'

'Now, don't talk in that way to me,' returned Flower. 'I don't like it. Grimes's is not above three miles off now.'

'Not so much,' said the shepherd. 'Two miles and a half will bring us to the house.'

'*I* know what the distance is,' said Drohne. 'But I'll go no further. I have made up my mind.'

'To what?' inquired Flower.

'To die!' said Drohne.

'Oh, that you are sure to do,' said Flower. 'But why not wait till you are sentenced? Now, come on; it is getting dark.'

'And if we don't reach the road before sundown, we shall be in the bush all night,' said the shepherd.

'You hear that?' said Flower.

'I do,' said Drohne.

'Well, and why kick up a row?' said Flower.

'Because I am ready to die,' replied Drohne. 'I may as well give up my life to you as to the Ketch.'

'Well, but I don't want your life,' said Flower. 'All I want is £100 for you from Gov'ment. I never saw such an un-reasonable brute as you are in the whole course of my life.'

'Take me dead!' cried Drohne.

'You would be so "high" in this weather,' said Flower; 'and I can't get the reward unless I produce your body. Now, don't be a fool. Come along. I hate being out all night in the bush.'

'Go on, *you*!' Flower called to Slobey.

Drohne prevented the advance.

'Now, look here,' said Flower. 'Look here, Drohne. It *is*, as far as your life is concerned, a matter of time, and if time is of no object to you, it is to *me*, remember – and if you won't go on, I'll do it at once.'

'Do it!' cried Drohne.

Flower levelled his carbine, and looked at Drohne.

'For God's sake!' screamed Bet and Sal.

'Have you made up your mind?' asked Flower, heedless of the screams of the women.

'I have!' said Drohne, firmly.

'That you will not go on? That you are to die by my hand, instead of the hangman's?'

'Yes!' said Drohne.

The women screamed again.

'Fire!' cried Drohne.

Slobey tried to urge Drohne forward. Flower did all he could to move his prisoner by persuasion, and then by force. But Drohne was a strong man, and he was successful in checking the march.

'Once more, I beg of you,' said Flower.

'Fire!' cried Drohne. 'Fire!'

Flower shot him through the heart.

The corpse, still handcuffed to Slobey, was carried on the horse, Flower holding it on the saddle from the near side.

The wailing of the women became deafening, and the faces of the shepherd and of Slobey were as pale as the lifeless visage of Drohne, whose head was now bent forward on the neck of his horse.

CHAPTER XXVIII

EMILY HAD ONCE more the misfortune to be robbed of the writing case, in which she kept the few trinkets that then belonged to her. The thief she fancied was a charwoman, whom she used to employ every Saturday to clean the windows and the furniture. Roberts affected to think so too, and gave Emily great credit for her acumen in guessing so correctly. 'But then,' he said, 'it would be madness to proceed against her without direct proof.'

Now, the truth was that Roberts had given the contents of that writing case to the woman in whose company he had been disgraced and degraded on the Paramatta racecourse. The brooch, which was his first present to his wife, was amongst the things the writing case contained, and a little gold pencil case, a present from her father on her twelfth birthday; a smelling bottle, the last gift from her mother; and a small seal which had belonged to her great-grandfather. In the absence of money, of which he was now very much in want, Roberts had bestowed these trifles upon 'the Enchantress'. And she used to *wear* the brooch; and the gold pencil case she appended to her watch chain, likewise the little seal, with which she used to seal numerous notes written for her by a young female, who was both her companion and amanuensis.

When Emily spoke to Mr. Brade of this distressing robbery he told her at once, but in confidence, his well-grounded suspicions – that her husband was the thief, and that he had given them to the woman who lived in the cottage at the top of Church Hill. Nay, Brade went further. He stated that he had seen the woman wearing the brooch, and the pencil case in her possession. But Emily, who was very clever in reasoning (all confiding and really virtuous women are), began to ask herself a variety of questions: *First.* Had not Mr. Brade an object in continually attempting to disparage dear Reginald? *Secondly.* Had not Reginald gone a dozen times to the police office and talked to the constables about the theft? Had he not come home and told her all that the constables had said? *Thirdly.* Had not dear Reginald cried with vexation when the theft was discovered? Was he not frantic to think that his first present should have been stolen from her? *Fourthly.* Had not dear Reginald gone into a violent passion with the charwoman, and ordered her never again to darken his doors? *Fifthly.* How could Mr. Brade have seen these things in the possession of the woman? Did he know her? How absurd of Mr. Brade to think she was such a perfect child! There was something so foolish, so simple, in men resorting to such trumpery artifices! Poor Reginald! When would the world see him in his proper light – as she did? But no wonder all the world seemed against him. It was nothing more than human nature. He was the handsomest man in the world; therefore, all the handsome men hated him. He was the cleverest man in the world; therefore, all the clever men detested him. He was the most open-hearted man in the world; therefore, the open-hearted would not praise him. He was the most witty man in the world, and, therefore—— Ah! She could see through it all! Dear Reginald! And to think that he should still swear by Mr. Brade, and fancy him such a great friend. Just like Reginald. He was so honest himself he could not fancy anyone otherwise until he had found them out. Poor dear boy! Brought up, as he had been, to every comfort and luxury – a scion of the aristocracy – the heir to a title – the idea that he should be in such a horrid country, surrounded by such people, and compelled to bear insult and contumely, and he not in a position to show his real spirit! But the day would yet come. It could not be far off; for the Almighty, though he often visited us with affliction for a time, was always just and merciful in the end!

It was thus Emily was in the habit of discoursing with herself whenever her husband was calumniated by Mr. Brade, or by anybody else.

CHAPTER XXIX

ROBERTS MIGHT HAVE earned at least five pounds a week by engrossing deeds, and other legal documents, but he could not bring his mind to work, and Emily did not press him to do so; for, 'poor fellow', she thought he had quite enough to distract him. Her own earnings, from needlework, were all they had to subsist upon, and these rarely amounted to more than thirty shillings per week. It was difficult to live upon this sum; but, somehow or other, Emily contrived to do so, for there are no economists in this world to be compared with women of lofty condition who have been brought up luxuriously, and have fallen into poverty by reason of their love. Their pride is aroused, and they can debar themselves, with a good grace, of comforts with which even the poorest can but ill dispense.

Emily now kept no servant. She did everything herself, even to washing her husband's linen, and scouring the floors and the passage of the cottage; and at night, when no one could see her, she would come out and whiten with a large sandstone the steps in front of the door.

One night, 'the Enchantress', with whom Roberts had been spending the day, flew into a violent passion, and stabbed him with a carving knife. The wound, which was in the left breast, bled profusely. It was not deep enough to be fatal, but, nevertheless, it was sufficient to arouse Roberts's fears. Pale and faint from the loss of blood he staggered to the arms of Emily, who screamed on beholding him in the condition in which he presented himself.

A man in a slouched hat, and muffled up in a cloak, he said, had aimed that blow at his life. When – he inquired of his wife – was this persecution to end?

Emily at once suspected Mr. Brade. Nay, she was convinced that this cruel attack had been made upon Reginald at Mr. Brade's instance, if he had not with his own hand inflicted that gaping wound.

A doctor was immediately sent for, and came at about one o'clock in the morning. He admitted that Roberts had had a very narrow escape, but expressed an opinion that he was in no sort of danger.

Emily watched by the convict's bedside during the night, and prayed fervently that the sufferer might be spared to her, and that his enemies might cease to pursue him. More satisfied than ever was she that all Mr. Brade had told her, and all that Flower had represented, were wicked and malignant falsehoods.

Mr. Brade called. When he heard the story from Emily's lips, of the assassin in the slouched hat and the cloak, he smiled in her face, and caused her to shudder at his want of feeling both for herself and her husband.

As soon as he could venture out alone, the convict, under pretence of 'going for a walk in the domain', wended his way to the cottage of the Enchantress. Roberts was too faithful to vice to be turned aside by a wound inflicted by a woman with a carving knife.

The Enchantress received Roberts with loving kindness, and pleaded drunkenness as an excuse for her violent cruelty. Roberts accepted the excuse and was satisfied with it; and, if possible, liked the Enchantress all the better, since she had left a mark upon him.

It was inconsiderate – perhaps indelicate – under the circumstances, on the part of the Enchantress, to ask Roberts for money at this meeting; but her wants compelled her to overcome her feelings. She wished for a new bonnet and some kid gloves.

How was Roberts to procure money? What was easier than to forge? With whose name could he take the liberty? Should it be a bill or a cheque? A cheque. And for how much? Twenty pounds. At first he thought of Mr. Brade's name; but he doubted if Mr. Brade had any balance in the bank. Then it struck him he would use the name of the attorney in whose office he had been employed. At length he decided on Lieutenant Colonel Wimbleton.

'He'll not dare to say a word about it when the forgery is discovered,' said Roberts to himself. '*I'll* manage that.'

And forthwith Roberts drew a cheque for £20 in favour of a 'Miss Burnes, or bearer', and signed it, 'Edward Wimbleton.'

Roberts could imitate any signature so exactly that it was hard to say which was the original and which the counterfeit.

The reader is requested to understand that Miss Burnes was under Colonel Wimbleton's protection; and Roberts was quite right when he calculated that the Colonel would hardly like to be cross-examined in a witness box, touching his relations with this lady, in the event of a trial in the Supreme Court.

Colonel Wimbleton's cheque for £20 was cashed imme-diately on presentation at the bank. And the Enchantress had her bonnet and gloves, and several other presents. And she and Roberts were very happy – as long as the £20 lasted.

CHAPTER XXX

'**I**s Major Grimes at home?' Flower inquired of a servant on arriving at the Major's door.

'Yes,' was the reply.

'Then just ask him to come out, will you?' said Flower.

The Major made his appearance, and Flower alighted from his horse.

'Good evening, sir,' said Flower.

'Good evening,' said Major Grimes.

'You don't recollect me, sir?' said Flower.

'No,' said Major Grimes.

'I had the honour of partaking of your hospitality a short time ago, sir,' said Flower. 'And I've brought back your shepherd, sir, and a queer lot along with him.'

'Indeed!' replied the Major, who was alarmed on recognising the features of the man who spoke to him; for on presenting the order for payment drawn by Millighan on the Lieutenant commanding the police, the Major had been made cognisant of the fact that he had been entertaining the notorious bushrangers, and not the military.[*]

'I'm Flower, sir,' said George. 'Commonly called *Mister* Flower – the person as the papers made drunk, and

---

[*] The mounted police were private soldiers, selected from her Majesty's Regiment of foot, then quartered in the colony.

drowned in the Hawksbury river. But the papers were in error, sir.'

'Oh! I see,' said the Major.

'No, you don't, sir. Excuse me,' said George. 'Don't be frightened, Major. It is all right, as I will soon explain to you. I have brought 'em in – the whole nest. One of 'em is a stiff 'un. That man there on horseback, held up by that individual, Tambourine Bet, is as dead as a doornail, Major. He compelled me to shoot him about an hour ago. He's dead, sir; but hardly cold, I take it. There's no mistake about my visit this time, Major. I am Flower – *George* Flower – frequently called *Mr.* George Flower – the king of traps. I'm as well known as the Governor, or the Chief Justice, or the Colonial Secretary. There's no mistake about me, Major.'

'Oh, I see!' said Major Grimes, whose alarm was now on the increase, for he did not believe a word Flower said, but fancied the gang had come again to rob his house, and perhaps murder himself and his family.

'I wish you *could* see, Major,' said Flower. 'It is all right, I assure you. I am George Flower, and have taken all that gang. Them two men as came here with me, and got tea and sugar and grog, are now dead. Send for a light, Major, and I'll show you one of 'em, and then you'll be convinced. And, then, here's your shepherd. He helped me to capture 'em. It is all right, I assure you, Major.'

The Major knew not what to think, but he ordered a light to be brought, and surveyed the whole party.

Drohne, whose looks were now horrible and ghastly, linked to his living comrade, was a striking proof that Flower's statements were true. But the sight turned Major Grimes sick at heart. And when he saw Flower (out of curiosity, apparently) plunge his forefinger into the hole the ball had made – when he heard him exclaim, 'Can't fathom it' – the Major almost fainted.

'Where can I put 'em, sir?' inquired Flower. 'For I must ask you to let me stay here tonight.'

'I will see,' said Major Grimes. And he sent for his overseer, who was a good deal surprised when he heard Flower's story, and saw the party he had brought in.

'Could you give us a barn,' inquired Flower, 'that would hold the men, the horses, and the ladies? These are ladies, you know, overseer, and capital police they make, too. And a few feeds of corn would not be a bad thing for the horses, overseer. Most of 'em belong to Gov'ment.'

It was decided that a stable should be devoted to the accommodation of the party. Flower then superintended the extricating of Drohne from Slobey – the latter, in reply to a question from Flower, having said that he should *not* like to sleep all night in such close contact with Drohne. Flower handcuffed Slobey's hands behind his back, and chained him, with a bullock-chain, to a ring attached to the manger in one of the stalls. And then – with the assistance of the woman and the girl – the latter holding the lantern over her head – Flower laid out the dead body of Drohne in the next stall, upon a broad sheet of bark, and borrowed an old white tablecloth from the overseer, and spread it beneath the corpse.

A third stall was set apart for the females. They were fastened with dog-chains to a ringbolt. This was done lest they might release Slobey during the night.

Flower, having made 'all snug,' betook himself to Major Grimes's kitchen, where he found mutton chops, fried cakes, and tea, all ready for him; and the pretty servant girl in attendance.

'You little dreamt, did you, Susey, when I was here last, talking to you so quietly, that I'd be back so soon? You had no idea then of the lay I was on, had you?' said Flower.

'No, sir.'

'Don't call me "sir", Susey,' said Flower. 'Call me your love, or your darling; but never say sir, or mister.'

The girl laughed, and presently remarked, 'And do you mean to say you shot that man?'

'Why not?' demanded Flower. 'Wouldn't he have cut your throat just as soon as look at you? Wouldn't he have taken hold of you so – and gone so?' He seized her round the waist, and rubbed his hand across her delicately formed neck.

'I say, what heavenly eyes you've got, Susan! Have you ever been in love?'

'No,' she replied. 'Have *you*?'

'Never till I saw you,' said Flower. 'And I have been in love ever since, and I'm now in love. Come, what do you say, Susan? There'll be a public house – fine trade – lots of money, pleasant company, gig and horse, and all that sort of thing. Be Mrs. Flower. Say the word at once.'

'You are joking,' said the girl, with a blush.

'Marriage is not a joke,' said George. 'And without being engaged to you, Susan, I could not think of asking you to give me a kiss, and I am dying to have one. Some folks are not particular in these matters, but I am, *very*. Upon my word, I never loved a girl till I saw you. Won't you, Susey? Won't you be mine?'

Susan sighed, and looked content. The truth is, that she was vastly pleased with Flower's fun the first day she saw him in the guise of a mounted policeman. His frank manner and his laughing face had won her heart, and she had often thought of him, and smiled at the recollection of many of his speeches to her.

'I shall be up all night, Susey,' whispered Flower. 'And when everybody is in bed and asleep, you come in here with a light; let it be at about two o'clock in the morning, and we'll settle matters and arrange about our marriage. Don't let us say anything more just now, for old Grimes will be coming presently; but don't you go away, Susey. I am very anxious for you to hear all I have been doing since we parted. Mind, at two o'clock you are to meet me here. Give us a kiss; nobody will see us. Thanks, dearest!'

Major Grimes came into the kitchen, and Flower gave him a succinct account of all that had transpired. Major Grimes was loud in his praises of Flower's bravery and skill, and no wonder Susan was already infatuated with her hero.

'Sir,' said Flower, when, with the permission of the Major, he had lighted his pipe, 'I have a great favour to ask of you.'

'What is it, Flower?'

'Why, sir, you see Gov'ment is very particular, and Gov'ment's quite right to be so, for frauds in dead bodies *have been* done by constables, and about eighteen months ago I lost five and forty pound by taking in a dead ranger to Hyde Park Barracks, who was so far gone that nobody could swear that it was the man for whom the reward was offered. I shot that man in fair fight at Bong Bong, and took him in a cart to Sydney; was thirteen days on the road, and after all lost the five and forty, and was laughed at by all the police office. Superintendent Heely said that I ought to have got a certificate from the nearest magistrate while the body was fresh and not putrefied. Don't you see, sir? Now by the time I get this body down to Sydney – and it will take me twelve days good – he must be gone; nobody could swear it was Drohne, you see, sir? So, what I want from you, Major, is the certificate. I want you, if you would be so kind, to go over the marks on the body, and compare them with the description in the *Gazette*. If you would be so kind, sir, I'd take it as a favour, for I should not like to lose £100. I'm a poor man, Major.'

Major Grimes did not relish the idea of this post-mortem examination, but it was a part of his duty to undertake it, and he therefore made no objection to Flower's request.

'Couldn't we make it a moral lesson, sir?' said Flower.

'How do you mean?'

'Why, sir, have up all your assigned servants, and let 'em see the dead, and hear me talk about him. I'm an awful public speaker, Major, whenever I have a good subject, and this is one, and no mistake. I could talk Wentworth or Wardell stone blind on it. I only want your people to look on – to see the corpse. I shall not say a word *to* them. I shall only address my observations to *you*, and they'll get 'em by a side wind, as it were.'

Major Grimes agreed with Flower, and ordered all his convict servants to be summoned. While he was absent, Flower filled his pipe again, and again made love to Susan.

Flower truly was a great orator by nature, and required no time to give his speeches the gloss of art, by 'thinking over' what he should say.

The convict servants – thirty-nine in number – were assembled in the stable; and Flower, carrying the lantern and smoking his pipe – followed by Major Grimes with the *Gazette* in his hand – jostled through the crowd, and approached the dead body of Drohne. He paused for about two minutes, and then began:

'That man, Major Grimes, weighs about fourteen stone, and the reward for him is £100 sterling, so that his carcass is worth about ten shillings a pound. Fine young man: broad chest, well limbed, and ribbed up. When that young man came to this country, transported for life, he had before him noble prospects, Major. He was assigned to a good master. If he had been steady for about five years he would have got his 'ticket'.* But he was lazy, and that made him discontented and restless. Laziness is at the bottom of all mischief, Major. So he took to the bush, and a pretty business he has made of it. He forgot that if the devil puts it into the heads of convicts to turn bushrangers, Providence checkmates the devil, by creating traps like George Flower, Major, and prompting Gov'ment to offer high rewards for 'em. Gov'ment's a glorious thing, Major. I respect Gov'ment. This young man has come to an ignominious end, as all must come to that doesn't know when they are well off. That man in the next box will be hung, and I can't pity him. Are lifers to bolt, laws to be broken, drays to be robbed, and gentlemen and ladies to be put in bodily fear? Civilisation is not such a jackass as to stand any of that sort of nonsense. It can't be done for the money. What's Bourke paid for?' (General Bourke was the Governor.) 'What's old Frank Forbes paid for?' (Francis Forbes, Esq., was the chief justice.) 'What's Thomson paid for?' (Thomson was the colonial secretary.) 'What am *I* paid for? Why, we are all paid for preserving the glorious majesty of resistless justice, and for nothing else, Major Grimes, and let them deny it who dare. But let us look at this man, sir. You observe, Major, 'wen on neck'. That wen would have been an awful eyesore to the Ketch, for look here, it would have bothered him. It

---

* Ticket of leave.

would have been in the way of the rope. That makes good the saying, 'That a man who's born to be shot will never be hanged.' Having observed that wen, sir, let me direct your attention to a mermaid on his breast. There she is, you see, with her curls, and likewise her fish's tail, and a looking glass in her hand. I don't believe in mermaids, for my part. Having docketed the mermaid, sir, will you be so good as to cast your eyes on his Anchor and Hope, and then these bulldogs, barking at a Bow Street officer? And now, with your permission, sir, we will turn him over, and look at the man hanging on his back. He must have had some idea of his fate before him, or rather behind him, as it happens. What a fool a man must be to have himself disfigured in that fashion! What does the *Gazette* say is the colour of his hair, sir?'

'Reddish brown,' replied Major Grimes.

'There it is, sir, reddish brown enough. And his eyes, Major?'

'Light blue.'

'There they are – light blue, look, sir,' said Flower, lifting the lids. 'And what else, Major?'

'Lost a front tooth.'

'There it is, or rather there it isn't,' continued Flower, pulling the clammy lips asunder. 'Have you any doubt, Major Grimes, that this is the body of Edward Drohne?'

'None whatever,' said the Major.

'Then that's all I require,' said Flower, and he rose from his knees, washed his hands in a bucket of water, and (without permission) wiped them on the corner of a smock frock worn by one of the audience.

'Now then, Major Grimes, the business being over, these parties may retire to their huts,' said Flower. 'I shall be to and fro all night, and there's no occasion for anybody else to watch this stable.'

~

'That's a nice girl, sir, that servant of yours,' said Flower, when himself and Major Grimes were returning to the house.

'Yes, she is, indeed,' replied the Major. 'And she's a very respectable girl, too. She's the daughter of a farmer who died near Bathurst a few months ago, very badly off, and left a large family behind him.'

'Indeed, sir? She's a currency lass, of course?' said Flower.

'Yes,' said Major Grimes. 'But she reads and writes very nicely.'

'That's a great gift,' said Flower. 'I have always felt the want of a good education. By heaven, Major Grimes, if I'd had a good education, I'd have been a sort of a Boney-Party. Now, look here, sir,' he continued, 'moral effect is a very fine thing, and does a great deal of good; but what's the use of moral effect if you don't carry it properly out? Gov'ment's very liberal. I don't complain of Gov'ment. But when a man like me, sir, rids a district like this, sir, of a gang of men like these, sir, ought not the district to mark its sense, sir, by coming forward and putting their names down for something handsome, sir? What would five hundred pound be to a large and wealthy district like this, compared with the moral effect that act would produce?'

'I agree with you,' said Major Grimes. 'And the district shall do it.'

'Thank you, sir,' said George. 'And if you ever have a dray robbed, you have only to drop a line to Mr. Flower, care of Pollack's public house, opposite the police office, and I will make it all right for you. You'll lend me a cart, sir, or sell me one for Gov'ment, and let that shepherd go with me tomorrow?'

'Oh, yes, by all means.'

'Then I'll bid you goodnight, sir. There's a bed all ready for me, I see, sir – here on the dresser. Goodnight, Major.'

Major Grimes bade Flower 'goodnight'. Proud man as he was, he involuntarily gave the thief-taker his hand when they parted.

~

At two o'clock – exactly at two – Susan, on tiptoe, stepped into the kitchen. 'Hush!' she said to Flower, who clasped her in his arms. 'Hush! The Major's room is not far off.'

~

The next morning Drohne's body was placed in a rudely formed coffin and put into a cart. Every precaution had been previously taken to make it as little offensive as possible. The shepherd was to drive the cart. Slobey and Sal were to sit upon Drohne's coffin, and Tambourine Bet, still dressed as a mounted policeman, was to ride beside Flower on horseback. All was ready, and it was now time to make a move.

'God bless you, my dear girl,' said Flower to Susan, who was weeping; 'I'll come back and marry you, you may take your oath. Goodbye!'

The Major came into the verandah to see the procession off, and say 'farewell' to Flower, who begged the Major not to forget the subscription, for the sake of a really good and wholesome moral effect.

The party set out for Sydney – the shepherd in high spirits at the prospect of getting a ticket of leave.

The cart had to be taken a roundabout way before it could reach the road. Just as they were ascending a hill, Flower's keen eye discovered a female form coming towards them. It was Susan, who had taken a short cut across the fields on purpose to join George Flower's party. She had a small bundle in her hand.

'Halloa, Susan!' exclaimed Flower. 'Where are you off to?'

'I am going with *you*.'

'Impossible! What would old Grimes say?'

'I don't care. You have stolen my heart.' (Susan began to cry.)

'Don't cry, my dear girl,' said Flower. 'Don't cry. Stolen your heart, Susan? Well, why can't you love me rationally, and have patience?'

'I must go with you, George.'

'Well, if you must – you must; but it is a very pretty business. Grimes will never get up the subscription; but he'll try and have me cashiered out of the police, instead. Don't cry, Susan.'

Flower got off his horse, slipped the rein over his wrist, held Susan round the waist in his right arm, looked affectionately into her face, and kissed the tears from her cheeks.

'Don't cry, my girl. It is all up with me. I have shirked the knot for a long time past, but I am caught at last. You have done it, Sue, and I am not sorry for it. Only fancy *me* married! Well, never mind, it can't be helped. Here, you – shepherd! Get down off that cart and get on this horse, and gallop up to old Grimes's, and tell old Grimes that Susan has bolted of her own accord and joined me, and that I am going to marry her. Tell him it is all right. Make haste. We will go slowly along the road, and you will soon overtake us. Give my respects to the Major. Off with you! Come along, Sue. Get into the cart, my treasure, and sit beside your George, in the flower of youth and beauty's pride. I'll make you a trump of a husband, you'll see, you beautiful darling. There now, don't cry any more. We'll be married in Sydney, and if that won't be another moral effect of this trip, why the devil's in it.'

About half an hour had elapsed, when the shepherd came galloping back with a note in his hand.

'Halloa!' said George. 'Here's an order for us to go back, I'm afraid. The old boy is in a rage.'

'But I'll not go back,' said Susan.

The note did not contain the order Flower expected. It informed him that Major and Mrs. Grimes trusted to his honour, and hoped he would lead a happy life with the excellent girl whose affections he had engaged. And there was a message for Susan. 'Tell her we forgive her, and hope to hear from her as often as she has time to write to us.'

'Hooray! I'm in for it at last!' cried Flower, when Susan threw her arms round his neck and clung to him, and kissed him, regardless of the presence of Bet, Sal, and Slobey, who were looking on.

A smile passed over the face of the manacled prisoner – who was now lying at full length beside the box which contained the body of Drohne – when he heard Flower's ejaculation and remembered how Flower used to talk to Millighan about 'that pretty girl at old Grimes's', and suggested to Millighan that he should not mind carrying her off to the den some fine moonlit night.

Flower's meeting with Sheriff, at Penrith, was a very amusing scene. The little horse knew his master's voice, and seemed mad with delight on again beholding him. And Flower hung about Sheriff's neck, kissed his nose, patted him all over, talked to him, and asked him a hundred questions.

'The cart is getting very unpleasant,' said Flower to Susan, 'and the shepherd shall drive the rest of the journey. You shall ride on Sheriff. I'll borrow a side-saddle. He'll carry you as quiet as a dog, and I will ride beside you on this big horse of Gov'ment's.'

CHAPTER XXXI

DEAREST BELOVED!
I am going to dine this evening with my friend, Brade. I am going there now. Brade's cabriolet will be at your door at half past five, and the groom will lead the horse, and bring you in the cabriolet to Brade's villa. Make yourself look very smart, Emmy, dearest. We dine at seven; but be ready to leave home at half past five.

Ever your affectionate,

REGINALD.

Emily was very wretched when she read this note; but, fearful of offending her husband, she made preparations accordingly. She washed and ironed a lace collar, and, ill as she could afford it, bought a new neck ribbon, and a pair of pale kid gloves; and she re-trimmed her straw bonnet, and mended her worn-out parasol.

At half past five precisely, Mr. Brade's cabriolet was at Emily's door. Emily was barring the shutters and the back door, when George Flower, who had left his party in the 'cells' of the police office, made his appearance on horse-back, accompanied by Susan, on little Sheriff.

'Get off, Susan,' said George, 'and let me take you to Mrs. Harcourt, and hear what she thinks about you. Stop a moment. I'll help you off.' Flower lifted his bride elect from the side-saddle, and placed her on the ground.

'What! George Flower?' exclaimed Emily. 'Why, they said you were drowned!'

'Oh, no, not yet, Mrs. Harcourt,' said George. 'I'm still living, and I'm going to be married. This lassie has managed to hook me.'

'Indeed, I'm very glad to hear it. Pray, sit down,' said Emily.

'Her name's Susan,' said Flower. 'She's a currency lass. Pretty girl, isn't she? And she's as good as old gold. Arn't you, Sue?' He placed his hand affectionately on the girl's shoulder, and looked into her lovely, honest face.

'How dreadfully sunburnt you are, George,' said Mrs. Harcourt. 'And you look quite haggard and weary.'

'Yes; I have had a good deal of anxiety of late,' said Flower. 'But it will be all over soon. Won't it, Sue? I shall now have some rest, I hope, in the snug little home I mean to make for myself. Where's the Captain? How is he getting on?'

'He is at Mr. Brade's, and I am going there to dine, and fear I shall be late; but you'll come and see me tomorrow,' said Emily; and she began to pull on her gloves, and express her sorrow to Susan that she was compelled to go away.

Flower rose from his chair, and surveyed Emily from head to foot.

'That's Brade's cab at the door,' said he. 'I thought I knew it.'

'Yes,' said Emily. 'He has sent it to take me to the villa.'

'Has he? How good of him! How came you to be acquainted with Brade?' Flower asked.

Emily explained, and informed Flower that Reginald and herself had dined at the villa one Sunday, and that Mr. Brade had since been in the habit of calling.

'Does he come here with your sanction? Is it your wish that he should come here?' inquired Flower.

'Why, to tell you the truth, George, I would rather that he stayed away; and I am grieved at the thought of now going there; but then, you know how poor Reginald is situated; and Mr. Brade being a magistrate, we dare not give him offence.'

'Oh! that's it, is it? Go into your room, Mrs. Harcourt, and take off your bonnet immediately.'

Flower drew himself up, and spoke in an imperious tone of voice to the lady. The expression of his face at that moment reminded her forcibly of her own father's, when he was in a passion. Flower's lips were quivering, and the veins in his neck swelling to an unusual size, while his eyes seemed to dart fire. Even Susan was alarmed when she beheld that fiendish look.

'Go to Brade's villa? By heaven you shall not!' he continued. 'I know Brade, and liked him; but as to allowing him to come near any woman for whom I'd a regard, I'd cut his throat first. I now see why he wanted to get me out of the way, the villain. But thank God, I have come in the very nick of time to disappoint him, and thwart his diabolical purpose. Take off your bonnet! Go you shall not! I will go instead of you, and give Brade a section of my mind.'

'But remember, George, Mr. Brade is a magistrate,' said Emily.

'What do I care for that? I am not in Brade's power.'

'But Reginald is,' said Emily.

'No, he is not,' said Flower. 'I can smash Brade. He is in *my* power.' Rushing into the street, Flower ordered Mr. Brade's groom to take the cabriolet away, and tell his master it was not wanted.

'Let nobody say there's nothing in dreams,' said Flower, when he returned to Emily's presence. 'I dreamt in the bushranger's den that I saw with my own eyes what my coming here has prevented happening. Let Susan remain with you, please, till I come back. I'll not be very long away.'

Flower's looks, voice, and manner now carried Emily back to the days when she was the joy and the pride of Orford Hall. His face was now the image of her father's. Agitated beyond description, the unhappy woman burst into tears. She was glad that Flower had returned, and yet she feared that his violence with Mr. Brade would entail some disaster on her husband.

Susan was full of the glorious achievements of George; but Emily listened to them with a tame ear, for her thoughts were engrossed in compassing the question, 'How will this matter affect poor Reginald?'

On arriving at Mr. Brade's villa, Flower was struck with the stillness of the place. Although the magistrate kept a number of servants, not a soul was to be seen. On hearing the sound of a horse's hoofs, Mr. Brade came out into the verandah. When he beheld Flower, he stood aghast. He believed him to be dead: for Flower had enjoined Major Grimes not to mention the capture; and he contrived to bring his party into Sydney without being recognised upon the road.

'Is that you, Flower?' said Mr. Brade.

'It is,' said George. 'Is there nobody to take my horse to the stable?'

'I'm afraid there is not,' replied Mr. Brade. 'My rascally servants have all gone away.'

'Then I will tie the nag to the fence,' said Flower. He did so; and placing his hands in his pockets, and walking boldly up to the magistrate, looking him full in the face, and becoming red with rage, Flower said, in a measured tone of voice, 'Are you not a cowardly villain?'

'What do you mean, sir?' said Mr. Brade, pale with fear.

'Why do you turn white and cower under my eye? Why do your hands shake? You are all alone! No one to come to you if you scream for help! None to save you if you implore for mercy from a strong ruffian! You expected an innocent lamb, you wily wolf, and you find yourself face to face with a roaring lion.' And seizing Mr. Brade by the arms, Flower pinioned him with his back to the wall, glared hideously at him, grinding his teeth while he foamed at the mouth, and the saliva ran down either side of his finely chiselled chin.

'Release me, Flower!' gasped Mr. Brade.

'You knew she was a lady. You knew she was an object of pity, such as the world never saw before. You knew that the end of her visit here today would have been her death – that she would have killed herself. And yet you——'

'Release me, Flower!'

'Don't speak, or I'll take your life here, and spare you the disgrace and misery I am going to bring upon you. I will see you, before three months have passed away, walking about the streets of Sydney in ragged clothes, and your toes peeping through your boots. You shall be starving, and compelled to pick up the half-crown I will throw to you, just as I would throw a bone to a hungry dog. You shall be turned out of your office, and forbade to come near Government House. Your friends will not dare to countenance you – mark my words – you cowardly villain! And in your poverty and wretchedness, your vanity shall not be consoled by the reflection that your name has been coupled with that of the lady you expected here this evening. No, you shall not have that satisfaction. Good evening to you, Mr. Brade.'

CHAPTER XXXII

WHEN FLOWER LEFT Mr. Brade he went forth in quest of Roberts. He knew all Roberts's old haunts, but he could not find him at any of them. From a woman, however, Flower learnt of Roberts's disaster on the racecourse, and of his being stabbed by 'the Enchantress'. To her cottage he therefore repaired, and placed his ear to the shutter. He heard Roberts's voice. He was teaching the woman how to play double dummy.

Flower knocked at the door, and as soon as it was opened he forced his way into the room.

The Enchantress had never had the pleasure of Mr. Flower's acquaintance, and she stared first at him and then at Roberts, who appeared, on observing his late master, extremely uncomfortable.

'How do you do, Captain?' said Flower, holding out his hand.

'Quite well, thank you, Mr. Flower,' said Roberts, giving his hand to George. But when Roberts wished to withdraw his hand he felt it detained, and presently he roared with the intense pain which the iron grasp of George Flower's fist occasioned him. It seemed as though his hand were a vice; the knuckles and the bones of the fingers were cracking under that awful pressure; his rings entered his flesh, and one of them was broken.

'Don't make such a noise,' said the Enchantress. 'You will have all the police here.'

'My dear madam, *I* am all the police,' said Flower, 'and a pretty scrape you will get into for harbouring a convict, contrary to an act passed by the Governor in council. I am sorry to deprive you of this gentleman's company, but he must go with me, unless you will permit me to punish him with this whip in your house. Yes, you really must give me leave.' And thereupon Flower seized Roberts and began to belabour him soundly.

'On second thoughts, I will not take him with me, madam,' said Flower. 'I could not trust myself alone with him tonight. He may remain with you till two o'clock in the morning, and at that hour he may go home to his wife, and tell her that he has been at Mr. Brade's villa, on the South Head road.'

'And are you really Mr. George Flower?' said the Enchantress. 'Well, I have often longed to see you. I heard you were such a handsome man.'

'And so I was before I became so sunburnt,' said Flower. 'I hear that you went to the races with my friend the Captain. While the Captain scrapes the mud off my boots, oblige me, madam, with the whole story, and I'll say nothing about finding a convict in your house at this hour of the night.'

Roberts did not require to be told twice to remove the mud from Flower's boots; and the Enchantress, seeing him so employed, and knowing full well the extent of Flower's power, related the story, while Flower smoked a pipe, and drank a bottle of pale ale which the Enchantress produced.

CHAPTER XXXIII

FLOWER MARRIED SUSAN Briarly, and resigned his appointment in the police office. He took a public house, and Emily painted his sign board in oils – a portrait of his famous horse. The house was called 'The Sheriff's Arms'. Flower also became the proprietor of a livery stable, and engaged in boatbuilding; and in all these ventures he was remarkably successful. Abrahams, the Jew, used to advance him any sums of money he required at a moderate rate of interest, for Abrahams was under very peculiar obligations to Flower, and would not have offended him on any account. In short, George Flower was now one of the most prosperous men in the colony of New South Wales.

Mr. Brade was dismissed from the magistracy for improper conduct, which Flower brought to light, and was walking about the streets of Sydney, almost bare-footed, and without a shilling in his pocket; and sure enough, Mr. Brade *did* receive money from George Flower's hand – not half a crown, but a five pound note. And Flower paid his passage to England, after reluctantly forgiving him the offence of which he had been guilty.

There was a constable who owed much to Mr. Brade, and he fancied that Roberts was the cause of his patron's ruin. He therefore brought to the notice of the bench that 'this convict, assigned to his wife, was seldom at home with his mistress', and that he was 'in the habit of staying out all night'. The bench regarded this as extremely improper, and the constable was ordered to apprehend Roberts on the next occasion that he found him in the streets, or in a public house at a late hour. Soon after this, Roberts and the Enchantress were drinking together, and playing cards, at about two o'clock in the morning; and on the constable breaking in upon them, the Enchantress assaulted the constable, and he, therefore, not only took Roberts into custody, but the woman also, and both were locked up in the cells.

The next day, Emily was summoned to appear. She came, in fear and trembling, and beheld her husband in the dock – and beside him the Enchantress, who nodded familiarly to Emily, and then told 'Reginald' to 'cheer up'. When Emily heard the deposition sworn to by the constable, and observed that her husband was silent when the magistrate asked him what he had to say in his defence – when she found that he could not, or would not look at her – when she heard the Enchantress abuse the magistrate, and tell him that 'Charley' was a much finer gentleman than *him* (the magistrate), she was deprived not only of power, of speech, but of reason.

'Have you anything to say, madam?' inquired the magistrate.

Emily stared at him, and sank into a chair. At this moment Flower came into the office, and took the unhappy woman away.

The bench were of opinion that the prisoner's services should be withdrawn from his wife and resumed by

Government. Judgement was delivered accordingly, and Roberts taken from the dock, and led to Hyde Park Barracks, where he was divested of his blue frock coat and tasteful necktie, his fancy waistcoat, drab pantaloons, wellington boots, black beaver hat, and lemon-coloured kid gloves; and clothed in a suit of coarse canvas apparel, consisting of a smock frock and trousers, with the letters H.P.B. (Hyde Park Barracks) and two broad arrows painted on various parts of either garment. In lieu of his white linen shirt, a coarse blue cotton garment was given to him, and he was fitted with a pair of 'slop' boots, with huge hobnails in the soles and heels. The cap he was required to wear was made of black cloth, and shaped like an old-fashioned nightcap with a large button on the top. He was made a messenger, and his duties were to carry letters from the superintendent of police to the various public offices.

Emily was now perfectly satisfied of the truth of all that she had previously disbelieved; but still, she could not banish 'the unhappy wretch' (she so spoke of him) from her gentle mind. She no longer desired to see him, or to speak to him; but since he was her husband, and she had loved him, she could not utterly abandon her interest in him. She was now living under the roof and under the care of George Flower and his wife, who frequently suggested to her the advisability of returning to England, and claiming the forgiveness of her parents. But Emily's invariable reply was, 'Not so long as that man lives.'

CHAPTER XXXIV

FLOWER BOUGHT TWO vessels – a ship and a brig. The ship was sent on a whaling expedition; and the brig, with a gang of men, was sent 'sealing' to Macquarie Island. In six months, both vessels returned – the ship laden with sperm oil, and the brig with 7,000 skins. The value of the two cargoes was £37,000. Such luck had never been heard of; and Flower, like a prudent man, sold all his property, and invested the proceeds in the Bank of New South Wales, and lived upon his dividends, which were rather more than five thousand pounds a year.

Roberts's first forgery in New South Wales had been so successful that he was tempted to take a loftier flight. He conceived a noble project. He was to obtain a very large sum of money – purchase a vessel in the name of some 'free man' – have her fitted out as a whaler – and in her get to America or the Cape of Good Hope.

There was a convict in Carter's Barracks called Sly – a shipmate of Roberts – who was an engraver – a very clever man in his trade; a man who had successfully copied the plate of a provincial bank, and had paid, or rather was paying, the penalty for so doing. Roberts had a conference with Sly, and Sly said that 'the plate of the Bank of New South Wales would be mere child's play' to him.

Roberts and Sly forthwith 'collaborated', and between them produced a work of astounding merit, so far as success was concerned. Sly did the engraving, and Roberts the signatures of the directors and the secretary. They made five hundred £20 notes, and gradually cashed them. Amongst other signatures of bank directors, Roberts, with a laugh upon his lips, used those of George Flower and Robert Wardell.

A convict, who had been formerly a commander in the Royal Navy, was now consulted about the vessel, and the means of escape. He suggested a fast-sailing schooner, then for sale, and 'lying off the Queen's wharf'. The boat was purchased, well stored with provisions, and all were ready for embarkation.

Three casks with false tops, covered with biscuits, were constructed to hold Roberts, Sly, and the naval gentleman, until the vessel was 'safe outside the Heads' – the harbour of Port Jackson. There was now nothing whatever to stand in the way of their escape from the colony, except Roberts's evil propensity. He must needs invite the Enchantress to share his wild fortunes in what he was pleased to call America – 'the mother penal country'. The Enchantress said she would, and Roberts then laid bare the whole of his heart, and informed her of what the reader is already in possession, touching his design to *escape*. But the woman did not keep her word. She gave notice to the police, went on board the schooner, and pointed out the three casks of biscuits in which the convicts were sitting, and peeping, respectively, through the bungholes.

The moment they were detected, each wanted to turn 'king's evidence', and convict the other two. But the Custom House officer who was on board, and who had some voice in the matter, very properly observed, 'Well, but you can't all three be king's evidence – draw lots for it.' This was done. A pipe-stem was broken into three unequal pieces, and the ex-naval hero was the lucky man – he drew the longest piece.

The forgery part of the business had not yet transpired, and Roberts had in his pocket a quantity of the £20 notes, and with these he purchased his release from the constable who had him in charge, and who permitted Roberts to knock him down and run away, while Sly was being conveyed to the jail by another constable whom he had not the means of bribing.

Sly was hanged, and Roberts made the best of his way towards Bathurst, where he joined two other runaway convicts of desperate character – men who (to use the colonial trope) had ropes around their necks; and, ere long, Roberts was the captain of the gang, which his fears induced him to increase until it numbered seven. At the head of this gang, or rather in the rear of it, Roberts committed several highway robberies, and in more than one instance wilful and wanton murder. Large rewards and conditional pardons, as usual, were offered for the apprehension of these bushrangers, but still they contrived to remain at large, and carry on their depredations with vigour and daring.

CHAPTER XXXV

O NE MORNING, FLOWER read in the *Australian* newspaper the following paragraph: 'The notorious Roberts, the confederate of Sly, who was hanged for the forgery on the Bank of New South Wales, is one of the gang of bushrangers whose deeds have recently occupied so much of our space. He was recognised by a bullock driver in charge of a dray belonging to Captain Raine, of Bathurst, which dray was robbed of sundry stores about a fortnight ago.'

Flower had given up business of every sort and kind, and was now living quietly in a villa which he had built on a lovely spot of land overlooking the ocean. It was near a place called Bundye Bay, and not very far distant from the famous bay (Botany) whence the colony of New South Wales has derived its disagreeable (from association) cognomen. Emily was still under the protection of Mr. and Mrs. Flower. Indeed, it was owing to her determination not to quit the colony so long as her husband was alive that Flower remained in the South, for he now panted to put foot again on the soil where he was reared, and stand on Yewbray Bridge, once more, and say, 'I would do it again tomorrow. He robbed my sister of her virtue, and he broke the old woman's heart, as well as the dear girl's.'

It was in a strange frame of mind that George Flower strolled down to the beach which bounded his domain, and faced the strong wind, which blew in his face and tossed about his long thin hair, and sent the monster waves hissing and creaming to his feet.

'Roberts a bushranger!' said Flower, contemptuously looking over the breakers at the troubled main beyond them. 'Roberts a bushranger! Defying the police! What has bushrangering and the police come to, at last? What would Donahough or Millighan say to this? Or Webber, or Alfred Jackson? Brave men who have died by this hand! I would take Roberts, armed to the teeth, as he would be, with no other weapon than a horsewhip, or a soldier's cane! You tell me that I could *not*,' said Flower, talking to the winds and the waves, and knitting his brows, and compressing his lips. 'I could not? I *will*. I swear – to you I swear, I *will*!'

Flower turned round, walked hastily home, went into the stable, kissed Sheriff, and smiled at the scars which decorated the gallant little animal.

'I owe all my fortune to you, Sheriff, my little dear,' said Flower, embracing his horse. 'If it had not been for you, Sheriff, I should have been killed *many a time*. Come along, my darling, let us have another brush. We'll go out together on a spree, as it were, and tell Susan we are going to see a flock of sheep that's to be sold at Bathurst. Riches have not made either of *us* fat, Sheriff – have they? But, my honour, you are getting as grey as a badger, and I'm getting one or two in my whiskers. Can't you kick, old boy, as hard as ever?' Flower touched Sheriff in the ribs, and the panel of the stall, on which the horse instantly left the imprint of his hoof, very loudly responded to the question.

That night Flower told his wife and Emily that he was going up to Bathurst to look at a farm which he thought of buying, and next morning after breakfast he took an affectionate farewell of them, and rode Sheriff quietly along the road to Paramatta, calling, as was his wont in former days, at every public house to have a few words with the landlord, the landlady, or the barmaid. And Flower took the opportunity of paying, with interest at twelve per cent, a number of scores which had been standing against him, and had escaped his memory for several years past. From Paramatta, Flower rode to Penrith, and from Penrith, in one day, he went to Bathurst – a distance of ninety miles. It was to the house of Major Grimes that Flower guided Sheriff. The Major was delighted to see him again, and so was Mrs. Grimes. But his host and hostess could not prevail upon him to go into their sitting room.

'No, Major; no, Mrs. Grimes,' said Flower. 'Riches doesn't alter rank; give me something in the kitchen, and come there and let me talk to you. The first time I came here I carried off some of your tea and sugar, Major, and the second time I carried off dear Sue. So you see I have been to you a regular robber.'

When Flower made known the *reason* of his visiting the Bathurst district again, Major Grimes was astounded, and so expressed himself.

'Ah, but you see, Major, it is not a matter of money with me now,' said Flower. 'It is a matter of passion and feeling. I cannot tell you all that is in my breast. But it must be; I must take this fellow and his gang, and you must help me.'

'How?' inquired Major Grimes.

'Why, you must give me a man and a horse, and you must make Captain Piper do the same, and all the other settlers who have had drays stopped and robbed. I want about six plucky men, all well mounted. Gov'ment's a fool for going to the expense of mounted police. You ought to learn the value of combination, and how to protect yourselves. You can club up to get rid of the blacks, when they spear your cattle or steal your sheep. Why can't you capture your own bushrangers? Why, hang it, the rewards would more than pay for the loss of time, and look at the inducement that a ticket of leave would be to your servants engaged in the affair.'

'I see,' said Major Grimes. 'But had we not better speak to the officer commanding the mounted police?'

'No, no,' said Flower. 'I wish to teach you settlers, and the Gov'ment, and bushrangers, a great moral lesson. I want to make you more independent and secure – bushrangers less numerous and daring – and Gov'ment more economical and sensible.'

CHAPTER XXXVI

FLOWER CARRIED HIS point. Every settler whose drays had been recently robbed was called upon, and each contributed a man. Some volunteered to take the field themselves; but to this Flower, for good reasons, no doubt, objected.

It was amusing to see Flower, mounted on Sheriff, putting his small force through its various evolutions, in a paddock fronting Major Grimes's parlour windows. The great difficulty that he had to overcome was making the stock horses stand fire.

All this was at last accomplished, and one fine frosty morning the force, with its leader at its head, moved out for action. Information had been gleaned by Flower of the enemy – located some eleven miles from Major Grimes's, and not very far distant from the den which has been already described in this narrative. No general officer ever knew better than George Flower the value of accurate intelligence – touching not only the enemy's position, but his strength, weakness, and resources. On all these points, Flower was thoroughly informed. From long experience he could guess the very hour a gang would be on the move – what direction it would take – and what would probably be its sport, or object of plunder; and upon this occasion his calculations were *marvellously* correct.

After riding eight miles there were seen, in the distance, six or seven men on horseback. 'These are they!' cried Flower. 'Now, my lads, be steady. When I tell you to charge, out swords and at 'em. Never mind your pistols, and don't mind theirs; it is not easy to shoot a man from the back of a horse in motion, but it is the easiest thing in the world to cut one down from the saddle. Be steady! Here they come!'

The forces were within a hundred and fifty yards of each other. Roberts became alarmed at seeing so strong a party, and suddenly recognising Sheriff and his rider, he called aloud – 'It is all over with us!' – then turned his horse and galloped away, followed by his gang, in great confusion.

'Charge!' cried Flower. 'Charge!' This order was obeyed, and a hard contest, in speed, immediately ensued, for Roberts and his party were excellently mounted. Ere long they came to some very bad ground, which slackened the speed of the horses, and in a few moments the pursued and pursuers mingled and fought, hand to hand.

Three out of the seven bushrangers were killed. Amongst them was Roberts. Flower lost two men and received a rather severe blow on his head from the butt end of an adversary's pistol. Nevertheless, the victory was complete, and what Flower so eagerly desired, *'Charles Roberts, alias Reginald Harcourt', ceased to live.*

'Yes,' said Flower, gazing on the corpse of Roberts, while his companions were digging a hole wherein to bury their own dead, and that of the enemy. 'Yes, it *is* so. It *was* to be. Something always told me it *would* be so. I knew it. I felt it.' Then turning to another of the slain he contemplated for several minutes the features so recently sealed in death. What was Flower's surprise, his horror, on recognising the face of a woman whom he knew in former days – a woman named Ellen Leger. She had been transported for poisoning her father, and on arriving in the colony had been 'drawn' as a servant, by a gentleman in power and in authority, and with that gentleman she had remained for several years. She afterwards ran away, committed some offence, was apprehended, shorn of her long black hair in the Paramatta Factory, and from that hour became a very desperate person. She had been good-looking, nay, handsome, and the traces of beauty were still upon her face.

'Well, thank Heaven,' cried Flower, 'that it was not *I* who cut *you* down, my poor girl. I was very near doing it once today!'

The bodies were buried, and the captured prisoners and their horses taken to Major Grimes's. Flower did not accompany the cavalcade. He was overcome by a curiosity to revisit the spot where he fought Millighan a few years previously, and Flower wended his way to the old den.

Not a soul had been there since the day he left it.

On the limestone table was a pipe which had belonged to Millighan, and a clasp knife which was once the property of Drohne.

Of the fowls not one remained; but the pigeons still clung to the abode; albeit they were now very wild, instead of so tame that they would settle on the heads and shoulders of those who formerly fed them.

There was property still in that den – guns, pistols, swords, handcuffs, plated ware, saddles, &c. &c.; but Flower was not disposed to carry anything away, except the broken handcuffs, which the reader may remember had been filed from his wrist on the night of his first appearance in that locality.

From the den, Flower proceeded on foot to the top of the mountain, leaving Sheriff in an enclosure, eating some rich grass which grew therein.

'Yes, that is the rock,' said Flower to himself, pointing to a huge mass of limestone. 'Yes, that is it – this is the way.'

The awful stillness of the place had struck Flower when he was there talking to Millighan, but now it was even more striking, more awful. Had Flower's heart been susceptible of fear at that moment, and in that spot, would the passion have stolen over him. As it was, he could not help muttering, 'What is the matter with me? I feel very curious – what is it?' he asked of himself, grounding his double-barrelled fowling-piece, 'What is it? There's nobody here, and if there was, what do *I* care?'

'I care,' the echo answered him.

Flower started, and then smiled at himself for so doing. 'Susey, dearest!' cried Flower, at the top of his voice, and echo responded the last word.

'All safe?' cried Flower.

'Safe,' was the reply.

(The echo amongst these limestone rocks is something wonderful.)

At a slow pace, and with a reverential feeling, George Flower directed his steps to the spot where lay the bones of Millighan. He placed his gun beside a rock, and, unarmed, went to gaze on the relics of mortality which had thither attracted him.

There was the skeleton of the man, quite perfect. Corruption had rotted the flesh, and with the flesh the clothes had been consumed. The eagle had not visited the dead body, nor had the wild dog. There lay all that remained of the man, *as he fell* – the rusted musket by

185

his side. But mingled with the bones of the man were the bones and the skull of the dog – the little terrier, who had died of starvation and grief, near the master whom he loved so well. Fresh from a scene of slaughter, with human blood recently shed upon his hands and clothes, Flower sat beside the skeletons of Millighan and his dog, and relieved the heart of its heaving by shedding scalding tears.

'*You* were a man,' said Flower, staring wildly into the sockets which once contained Millighan's bright eyes. 'And you, poor dog, you were as clever and as brave as he was. Better to die with one you loved than live without him. *Dear* Nettles.'

Flower put his hand gently on the little dog's skull, but did not disturb the position which, in the last moment, the dog had taken up on the breast of his master.

'What is this?' cried Flower. 'Here is the ball – the ball which flew from that carbine, and stopped the current of his life!' And inserting carefully his fingers between the ribs of Millighan's skeleton, he took up, and held between his forefinger and thumb, the fatal and slightly battered piece of lead.

Flower was in the very act of putting the bullet into his pocket, but something checked his hand; some mysterious power seemed to whisper 'No' – and Flower replaced the bullet with the same care, lest he should disturb the bones, that he used when he removed it.

Millighan, when he fell, had in his pocket a small silver flask, which contained spirits. On this the worms could not banquet, and there it was – blackened, but still perfect. 'Into this I will put his epitaph,' said Flower, 'and some day or other, when these remains may be stumbled across, those who find them shall not suppose he was some black fellow.' So Flower wrote on a piece of paper with a pencil the following words: 'This man's name was Millighan; he was killed in a fair fight with one George Flower. The dog's name was "Nettles". George Flower wrote this himself. My handwriting is well known.'

Grief, as well as ardent spirits, has its intoxicating properties; and Flower lost sight of the fact that the day was drawing to a close. For full three hours he remained beside the skeleton – speculating, as more educated philosophers have done before him, upon matters which we have no inclination to discuss.

When Flower left the skeletons of Millighan and the dog, it was almost dark, and *quite* dark before he arrived at the den. To find his way to Major Grimes's was utterly impossible. In the broad daylight it would be far from an easy matter, for the trees which had been marked had, in the course of nature, shed their bark several times since Flower was an inhabitant of the den. Flower, therefore, was compelled to stay in the den all night; into the den he took Sheriff, and, in the absence of any other companion, talked to the horse incessantly, and asked the little animal, several times, whether he would not rather die with him (Flower), as Nettles had done with Millighan, than live with any other master?

At about twelve o'clock Flower became very hungry. He had not tasted food for eighteen hours. He next became faint, then ravenous, and would have given any sum of money for even a biscuit and a glass of wine. He made a fire (as the Aborigines do, by rubbing two pieces of dry stick together till they ignite), and was sitting over it, thinking how he could satisfy the cravings of hunger, when suddenly he got up, lighted a wax candle (there were several pounds of wax candles in the den), and searched about in the desperate hope that 'something to eat' might be discovered. There was a box of macaroni, which with his own hands Flower had taken from the dray of Captain Piper; but it was rotten, and full of weevils, and when handled, it became like 'seconds flour'. He mixed this with water, kneaded, and was frying it, when he heard the pigeons cooing in their cote.

That horrible impulse of our nature which always steals over us under similar circumstances now stole over Flower, and he was bent on taking the life of one of those creatures which have been 'sanctified to our uses'. He put down the frying pan, ejaculating, 'By Jove! A grilled pigeon!'

Flower went out stealthily from the den, put his hand into the cote, and withdrew a plump bird. He brought it into the den with the intention of wringing its neck, but – lo and behold! – he recognised 'poor, old Moses', a pigeon so christened by the women; and around the bird's leg there was a gold earring.

'I would not hurt you, or any of your numerous family, for the whole world,' said Flower, releasing the patriarch pigeon, which, strange to say, seemed not afraid of George Flower; for, instead of flying away in terror, he partook of the macaroni pancake, dipped his beak into the water, and pouted about the table, in apparently an ecstasy of satisfaction.

The next morning, at daybreak, Flower saddled Sheriff, and rode to Major Grimes's. His absence had caused great alarm, and people had been despatched in all directions to search for him, for the Major was fearful that Flower had been 'lost in the bush'.

The bushrangers were 'given up' to the men who had assisted in their capture, and Flower took leave of Major and Mrs. Grimes, after thanking them over and over again for not being angry with him for taking away from them 'the best-hearted and prettiest girl that ever breathed'.

CHAPTER XXXVII

THE DEATH OF Roberts and the two others who fell by his side, and the capture of the remainder, were published in all the papers (the *Sydney Gazette*, the *Monitor*, and the *Australian*). But Mrs. Flower and Emily knew nothing of this; for Flower, previous to setting out upon his expedition, had 'stopped his subscription', and had given orders to his servants that no newspaper was to be allowed in the house during his absence. It would be difficult to say which of the two welcomed Flower back the more heartily, Susan or Emily.

~

'Why are you out of sorts, George?' said Susan, when Flower, after dinner, was sitting silently over the fire, smoking his pipe. 'You have been away for more than a month, and, now that you have come back, you won't speak a word.'

'Go to bed, Susey, dear,' said George, with a kind look, which Susan understood. 'I want to have some conversation with Mrs. Harcourt.'

Susan lighted her candle – bade Emily good night – and left the room.

'Now look here,' said Flower, 'there's no use in hesitating. I am going home to England, and mean to take Sue. Will you go with us, or not?'

'Not so long as that man lives.'

'He does not live: he is dead!'

Emily stood up. Her face became very pale; she trembled, and said, 'Dead! Is Reginald dead?'

Flower, observing her emotion, dropped his pipe, caught her in his arms, and cursed himself for breaking, so abruptly, intelligence of a nature which he ought to have known would shock the feelings of a sensitive woman.

A scene ensued – Susan was called – and Emily conveyed to her room, in a state of insensibility.

The shock over, Emily's mind experienced a relief, when she reflected on Roberts's death. Her chief anxiety, of late, had been lest he should perish by the hands of the public executioner.

Emily now no longer objected to accompanying Flower and his wife to England, though she feared that her parents would never forgive her, or listen to any of her entreaties.

Flower sold his bank stock and houses, and the proceeds were £51,000. With bills upon England for this amount, he embarked on board the old *Lady Jane Grey*. The stern cabins were engaged, and Emily had one of them – and a good-sized cabin, in the fore part of the vessel, was secured for Sheriff, whom Flower could not leave behind him.

Off Cape Horn the *Lady Jane* encountered very boisterous weather, and Susan, who was in delicate health, became seriously ill. Emily, who had of late gained strength and spirits, watched her with much care and tenderness, and thus repaid a portion of the obligations she was under to Susan's husband.

But, alas! Neither the skill of the surgeon, nor the attentions of Emily and of George could hold in its mansion the fleeting breath of Susan Flower. She died in the arms of her manly husband, and was committed to the troubled deep on the following afternoon.

For several days after the death of his wife, Flower never uttered a single word, or shed a single tear – nor could he be prevailed upon to take food. His cheekbones began to protrude, beneath his eyes came dark lines, and his face was as pale as that of a corpse. He sat down upon a chest, in his cabin, and there remained, in a perfect lethargy of woe.

Emily became alarmed, and did all in her power to rouse her protector, and console him. She, who had recently been as helpless as an infant, was now as active and intelligent as an experienced nurse; while he, who had lately been as strong as a young lion, was nerveless and childish in his overwhelming affliction.

Old Captain Dent, this voyage, had his wife on board. She was a motherly lady, who had seen much sorrow in her day, arising from domestic bereavement, and she hinted to Emily that if Flower could be moved to tears, his present mood would speedily disappear. Emily acted on this hint – took Mrs. Dent into Flower's cabin, and began to tell Mrs. Dent, in Flower's presence, of all Susan's good qualities: how kind and gentle was Susan, and how beautiful and good-natured.

At first, Flower did not heed Emily's discourse. There he sat, gazing on the floor, and wearing that peculiar vacant look which had overspread his countenance since Susan's death. But, at length, his ear drank in a few of Emily's words, and he regarded her intently.

Emily pursued the strain, and, ere long, 'the flood gushed forth' from that overcharged brain, and Flower was aroused to consciousness.

CHAPTER XXXVIII

AFTER A PASSAGE of four months, the *Lady Jane Grey* sighted the Lizard Light, and next morning the land was clearly visible. Flower and Emily were gazing on it from the poop, and experiencing those emotions common to all who have been for any length of time absent from their country.

'Where do you intend going when we land, George?' Emily inquired.

'To Orford Hall,' was the reply.

Emily shuddered, and remained silent for a few minutes.

'But I cannot go there,' said she, 'until I have written to my father and mother.'

'No,' said Flower; 'but you can go with me to a roadside inn that stands near Yewbray Bridge – or that used to stand there in my day – and there you can remain until I have seen your father, and heard what he has got to say.'

'And will you see him?' she inquired.

'Of course, I will,' said Flower. 'I wonder if he will remember me. He used to be very fond of me when I was a little fellow, and always took a great interest in my welfare. What awful changes we shall find in the neighbourhood! Prepare your mind for that, Mrs.——'

(Flower, since Roberts's death, never breathed any name when addressing Emily.)

'I am prepared for all,' said the unhappy lady. 'I am even prepared for the refusal of my father and mother to receive me under their roof. I am prepared to lead a life in England quite as unhappy and as cheerless as was that in New South Wales.'

CHAPTER XXXIX

A T GRAVESEND, FLOWER and Emily disembarked – and Sheriff, the first Australian horse that ever rounded Cape Horn. Sheriff was very stiff on landing, though in excellent condition: and he created no small amount of curiosity with those present; for Flower had brought home the identical saddle that Sheriff always wore on great expeditions, and it was now upon the little horse's back. It was not a pig's skin, but made out of the hide of a calf. Its flaps were not padded, but flush. The stirrup leathers were as black as ink, and very thin, though strong; the irons that were attached to them were so small that the toe only of a man's boot could get inside them. There was a sheep's skin spread behind the saddle, and fastened under the crupper. On this reposed sundry pairs of handcuffs, and a small chain. The bridle, too, was rather quaint; the headpiece was that of a gig horse, with the blinkers cut off; and the bit, a racing snaffle, as light (to use Flower's words) as a feather.

But if the horse and his trappings attracted attention, so did also his master.

Riches had not worked any change in either Flower's sentiments or dress. He still wore the uniform fustian shooting coat and fustian trousers (washed white), and the blue cloth waistcoat; boots, laced up the front, and a cabbage-tree hat, with a black ribbon; while around his neck was a blue silk handkerchief, tied in a sailor's knot.

Flower had become not only very 'colonial' in outward appearance, but in parlance he was peculiarly so. He had mixed a good deal with the blacks during his stay abroad; and in the colony (where the Aboriginal language, if it be not thoroughly understood by the European, nevertheless contributes sundry words and phrases which became current) it was all very well to use occasionally a little of it; but in England it was otherwise; and therefore, when Flower told a groom to give Sheriff some 'patter', he was driven to explain that 'patter' did not mean a thrashing, but 'grub'. So, also, when he used the word 'narang' (small) but 'bidgee' (good), the groom did not quite comprehend the gentleman's praise of his horse, which induced Flower to say, 'You stare at me as if I had just come from some outlandish country!'

A large carriage and post-horses were hired, and Emily and her boxes put inside. Flower took his seat in the rumble. They had only a journey of twenty miles before them.

When they neared the spot where they had been born, how strangely did the heart of each palpitate.

And now, every house, every tree, every lane became familiar to Flower's eye. And – yes, there was the bridge! Yewbray bridge!

There was the spot where the young Squire fell – and there was the little roadside inn, whither George Flower, on that morning, now twenty years ago, ran, and boasted of having done the deed!

'Stop!' cried Flower. 'Pull up here!'

Flower descended, and took Emily from the carriage into the inn. She was greatly agitated, and very pale; but Flower bade her take heart, make herself comfortable, and not talk to any of the people of the house.

The landlady did not recognise Flower, but he recognised *her*. She was a young unmarried girl when he left that part of the world. She was now the mother of eight or nine children. He longed to make himself known to the landlady, but contrived to master his inclination, and left the inn on foot. He went to the lodge where his family used to live. All were gone!

Flower paused for a few minutes.

'Ah! That's where I shall get the most information in the shortest space of time!' said Flower to himself; and he bent his steps to the churchyard, wherein he had often played as a boy, and where he had first learned to read.

Yes, there was told the tale. His mother was sleeping beside that sister whom he so dearly loved. But of his father, who always treated him and his sister with so much severity, there was no record. He knelt beside the grave, and placed his head on the stone which marked the spot where lay the dear ashes of his kindred; and he plucked some daisies, and placed them on the stone. He then strolled about the yard, and saw the graves of many whom he had left in the bloom of life – many a brave lad, and many a bonnie girl, with whom he was acquainted. Inside the church he then moved, to see what inroads death had made amongst the gentry. Yes, the gentry had suffered as much as the peasantry. Lord Waldane's monumental slab was there, and those of many other great folks whom he remembered. And there was cut upon a piece of white marble these words: 'In memory of Emily, wife of Edward Orford, Esq., of Orford Hall.'

'Then *he* is not dead,' said Flower, 'he is still living. I am sorry for Mrs. Orford; but why I know not, she never liked *us*.'

It was now evening, and Flower walked to Orford Hall, which stood about three quarters of a mile distant from the church. He inquired at the lodge if Mr. Orford was at home, and was answered – 'Yes.' He entered the house, and expressed to the footman a wish to see the master.

'What name?'

'Well, I don't see the necessity of giving my name,' said Flower. 'Tell Mr. Orford that a person has come to give him some information. Mr. Orford is a magistrate, I believe?'

'Yes.'

'Then go, and tell him what I have told you.'

The footman called to another footman, and saying, loud enough for Flower to hear, 'Keep this gentleman company until I come back,' he went into the library to deliver the message.

After an absence of a few minutes, the footman returned, and said, 'Walk this way,' and he conducted Flower to Mr. Orford's presence.

Mr. Orford had grown very old, infirm, and irritable. When Flower was announced, he was reading the Bible.

'Well, sir, and what may be your business?' he asked.

'It is private business, sir.'

'Shut the door, and go,' said Mr. Orford to the footman.

'You do not remember me, sir,' said Flower, when they were alone.

'No, sir; who are you?'

'It is more than twenty years ago since we met, sir.'

'Well, that may be. But who are you? What do you want? What is your business?'

'Sir, you knew not only me, but everybody belonging to me.'

Mr. Orford put on his spectacles and surveyed the intruder. He rose from his chair, with the assistance of his hands, approached Flower, who was still standing, hat in hand, and peered into his eyes.

'Good Heaven!' ejaculated the old man, placing his hands upon Flower's shoulders. 'My boy! Is it you, George?' And he clung to Flower, and clutched him by the elbows.

'You remember me now, sir?'

'Remember you? Forgive me for speaking harshly to you, my poor boy. How often have I thought of you, of late – longed for you to be here with me, to talk to me – and read to me. Why did you not write to me?' And the old man shed tears which fell upon the cuffs of Flower's shooting coat; and Flower, too, wept and loved the old man for his warm greeting.

'You will stay with me?' said Mr. Orford. 'You will never leave me, George? I am all alone here, with no one but these servants about me. Sit down, and tell me all that has happened to you.'

Flower obeyed Mr. Orford. He told him of his career in the colony, and of his circumstances – that he had returned with £50,000, and more, and how he made it. But Flower did not yet touch upon Emily.

'I wish I could tell you something,' said the old man.

'Do so, sir.'

'Not now, tonight, when everyone is in bed, fast asleep.'

'And I wish, sir, I could tell *you* something.'

'Perhaps you suspect it – know it?'

'What, sir?'

'My secret.'

'No, sir; I fancy not.'

'Then tell me, *what* is it you wish to say?'

Flower fell upon his knees, and said, 'For God's sake, Mr. Orford, forgive your only child!'

'I do,' cried the old man, raising him, 'I do – I did long ago, for it was a crime which will be pardoned in heaven.'

'Then may I bring her to you? She is not far from you, at this moment. I have protected her as though she had been my own sister, or my own child.'

'Her? Who?' inquired Mr. Orford, eagerly.

'Your only child, Emily, a wretched widow, who repents of her folly.'

'Are you mad?' said Mr. Orford. 'Or is this a dream? Emily lives? No – she is dead, poor dear. She died, without a friend to compose her limbs, and her mother——' The old man faltered, and wept afresh.

'I have been the protector of your daughter for several years past – up to this very hour.'

'How – her protector? Where?'

'In New South Wales. I have been to her a brother, though she is of gentle blood, and I am not.'

'Emily lives? Where is she? Conduct me to my child. Order the carriage.'

'Let me bring her here, sir.'

'Then haste – haste!' said the old man. 'What a strange world is this! This night, George, you shall know the truth!'

CHAPTER XL

FLOWER HASTED IN the carriage to the roadside
inn, where he found Emily in sore distress. She had
gleaned that her mother was numbered with the
dead, and so great was her grief, that the glad tidings of
her father's forgiveness did not stay her tears.

As soon as Flower left Orford Hall, Mr. Orford ordered
the servants not to come near him until they were called,
so that when Flower returned with Emily, there was not a
soul to be seen.

The poor penitent was conducted to the library, and
there the meeting with her father took place.

She knelt to the old man, and, with upraised hands,
craved his pardon; and he forgave her from his heart, and
placed his aged palms upon her aching head, and blessed
her, and sanctified the blessing with pious tears. And Emily
was once more under her own roof, and was installed the
mistress of that ancient abode. And that night she slept
in, or rather wandered about, the room which from childhood up to the unhappy date of her error had been hers.

And Emily heard from her father's lips that her mother
had, in her dying moments, forgiven her, and prayed for
her salvation in the world to come.

And that night Mr. Orford divulged to George the secret to which, in the morning, the old man had so mysteriously alluded. He told George that when he, Mr. Orford, was a very young man, he was wicked enough to engage the affections of a young girl whom his parents would not permit him to marry – that had he married her he would have been disinherited – that the fruit of this connection were two children, a boy and a girl – that Lord Waldane's gamekeeper, Edward Flower, had married the mother of these two children, receiving with his wife a marriage portion of several hundred pounds – that he, George Flower, was the son, and Bessy, whose wrongs he had avenged, the daughter; and hence that remarkable likeness which not only 'Bessy' but George Flower himself bore to Emily!

~

A few months passed away, and Flower began to feel lonely and miserable. He no longer cared for shooting and fishing. These sports had lost their charm with him. He fancied that he was looked upon with suspicion by persons with whom he made acquaintance; and it became tedious to him to explain to everybody who heard that he was 'an expiree' that he was 'not transported for thieving, or anything mean or low, but for justifiable murder'.

Flower engaged a passage for himself and Sheriff, and re-sought those shores whereon he had achieved so much renown, and where he was 'as well known as the Governor or the Chief Justice, and quite as much respected by honest men and feared by rogues'. He kept up a regular correspondence with Emily and her father, and frequently sent them Australian curiosities, such as kangaroos, emus, flying squirrels, parrots, and cockatoos; in return he received saddlery, cutlery, and other matters precious in his sight.

Mr. Orford died, and Emily succeeded to his estate.

Sometime afterwards, Emily was sitting in the drawing room, all alone, when a card was put into her hand.

'Sir Charles Everest!'

How Emily blushed. What scenes, painful and other, did the sight of that name recall!

Sir Charles took Emily's hand, and said to her, 'I will not release this till you promise to be mine. I have never ceased to love you, Emily, dearest, and I never shall cease to do so.'

Emily held down her head, and gave no reply – but she suffered him to retain her hand in his, and play with its small fingers. Presently, he raised it to his lips, and kissed it fervently. She accepted his proposal on the condition that he would never remind her or allude to the dark past. After a few months Emily became Lady Everest. And the evening of her life was tranquil and happy.

APPENDIX

Mrs. Stanley, la mère de Mrs. Stanley-Krasinska, avait perdu depuis peu d'années son mari, lorsqu'elle visit s'établir à Londres afin de perfectionner l'éducation de sa fille qui, annonçant des dispositions très-remarquables pour la musique, avait besoin d'acquérir un talent et de l'utiliser, la veuve et ses enfants n'ayant d'autre perspective de fortune qu'un héritage contesté. Un des fils (ils étaient deux) émigra au Canada avec un emploi du gouvernement: le second devint commis dans la cité, où, pour être plus près de son bureau, Mrs. Stanley et Eliza, sa fille, avaient loué une modeste maison.

Ce fut en 1813, au mois d'octobre, peu de temps après la bataille de Leipsick, que le jeune Stanley fit la connaissance d'un officier polonais du duché de Posen, venu à Londres en permission pour s'y guérir de ses blessures, se donnant pour aide-de-camp de Blücher, et se faisant appeler le comte Casimir Krasinski. Cet étranger était charmant de manières et le jeune Stanley le présenta à sa mère. Grâce à l'intérêt qui s'attache toujours à un brave qui porte un bras en écharpe et marche avec une béquille, Casimir Krasinski ne tarda pas à devenir intime dans la maison Stanley.

Il y prenait souvent le thé, amusait ses hôtes par l'histoire de ses campagnes et introduisait adroitement celle de ses ancêtres, avec la mention de l'espérance qu'il avait de rentrer dans leurs domaines, quand la paix remettrait tout le monde à sa place, sûr, d'ailleurs, de la protection de son général et même de celle du roi Frédéric-Guillaume, dont il avait préféré le service au drapeau de Napoléon.

Il montrait alors une carte topographique des terres paternelles, un arbre généalogique, des lettres de Blücher

et autres pièces en polonais ou en allemand qu'il tradui-
sait aux dames Stanley. Il était guéri depuis un mois et l'on
s'étonnait de ne pas le voir partir, lorsqu'il déclara son intention de se fixer en Angleterre si Miss Stanley consentait
à devenir sa femme, déclaration parfaitement accueillie de
la mère, de la fille et du frère, tous enchantés du charmant
Polonais.

Le 7 avril 1814, ce fut lui qui arriva triumphant auprès
de sa future et annonça l'occupation de Paris par les alliés.
"L'Europe," ajouta-t-il, "va changer de face, et ma fortune
aussi; mail il faut que je parte sans délai; il faut qu'avant
quinze jours je sois auprès de mon ancien général." Eliza
pâlit à l'idée d'une séparation; Mrs. Stanley versa des
larmes; mais Krasinski s'empressa de rassurer ses alarmes;
"Je serais déjà en possession de mes biens," dit-il, "que je
me croirais le plus lâche des hommes si j'étais ingrat envers
la tendre hospitalité que je reçus à Londres...si je ne tenais
les serments qui me lient à cette famille dont j'ai voulu
faire la mienne, – ou plutôt si j'oubliais cette affection
sincère que l'événement appelé de tous mes vœux ne
saurait étouffer dans mon cœur. La seule condition que
je suis forcé de mettre au mariage qui est encore ma plus
chère ambition, c'est qu'il soit immédiat." – Eliza lui tendit
la main en souriant; mais Mrs. Stanley pleurait encore.
"Je vous comprends," dit Krasinski, "vous pensez que je
veux vous enlever votre fille...Non; je prétends qu'elle
conserve sa mère et que nous vivions tous les trois dans
mon château dès qu'il me sera restitué. Je suis orphelin
et j'ai choisi une seconde mère en même temps qu'une
femme..." Bref, on admira le chevaleresque caractère de
l'officier polonais: on fut reconnaissant de sa générosité,
le mariage fut hâté, et au bout de quinze jours Krasinski

conduisait à Paris sa nouvelle famille. Les voilà dans un des hôtels où descendent les plus riches étrangers, et Paris à l'aurore de la paix en avait tout d'abord vu accourir un certain nombre.

Depuis cinq jours, Krasinski allait and venait de l'état-major prussien à l'hôtel apportant les nouvelles et disant combien son général avait été heureux de le revoir. Blûcher voulait aussi que Mme Krasinska et sa mère lui fussent présentées: le vieux vainqueur était si paternel qu'il exigeait que son aide-de-camp les amenât sans la moindre cérémonie, sans aucune parure, avec leurs robes les plus simples. "Ainsi," leur dit Krasinski, "vous êtes bien comme vous voilà, attendez-moi toute la soirée et je viendrai vous prendre dès que j'aurai accompli un message dont je suis chargé par mon général." C'était en dînant, au dessert, que Krasinski parlait ainsi, et il laissa sa femme avec Mrs. Stanley, languissant dans l'attente de son retour jusqu'à dix heures, impatientées de ne pas le voir revenir, tressaillant au bruit de chaque voiture qui s'arrêtait devant la porte de l'hôtel. Onze heures sonnèrent: Krasinski n'était pas revenu. Minuit, la plupart des étrangers de l'hôtel qui avaient été à des soirées ou au spectacle rentrent successivement. Tout à coup une clameur s'élève dans les escaliers et les corridors…Presque en même temps chacun s'apercevait d'un vol. Tous les appartements avaient été envahis, tous les tiroirs fouillés: les bijoux et l'argent n'y étaient plus. Rien de rapide comme les soupçons quand un voleur a fait son butin.

De l'un à l'autre on se répéta que voleur ne pouvait être que le comte polonais. Au milieu de l'inquiétude qui les agitait depuis deux heures, Mrs. Stanley et sa fille se voient accusées d'être les complices d'un malfaiteur…Ce qu'elles comprennent de la langue de ceux qui leur demandent ce qu'est devenu l'homme attendu par elles suffit pour les troubler et les accabler.

Bientôt un agent de la police survient, appelé par les plaignants. Elles voient fouiller leur chambre et reconnaissent alors qu'elles sont dépouillées comme les autres habitants de l'hôtel. Elles se réjouissent presque de cette découverte qui semble à la fois absoudre l'absent et attester surtout leur innocence: mais, tout au contraire, cette circonstance tourne contre elles: on s'écrie que la chose a été ainsi arrangée pour détourner le soupçon, et le soupçon s'acharne contre les deux dames anglaises. On les arrête, on les met on prison. Pendant deux jours elles espèrent en vain que Krasinski, dont la disparition leur semble une énigme, viendra en donner le mot...

Quand elles ont comparu devant le commissaire de police et sont acquittées, c'est pour se trouver isolées, étrangères, inconnues et suspectes encore, allant en vain à l'état-major prussien demander une audience du général Blücher et invoquant un nom qui devait être pour elles un talisman protecteur. Elles apprirent là que le général n'avait jamais connu Casimir Krasinski ni entendu parler de lui.

Elles s'adressèrent alors à l'ambassade anglaise et se virent réduites à accepter l'espèce d'aumône que l'ambassadeur leur accorda pour les mettre en état de retourner à Londres auprès du jeune Stanley, resté l'unique soutien de sa mère et de sa sœur. Pendant quinze ans, à travers toutes sortes de vicissitudes, longtemps pauvres, puis arrivant au gain de leur procès, Mrs. Stanley et sa fille avaient toujours devant les yeux l'image de set étranger qui était venu s'associer à leur destinée sous les dehors les plus romanesques pour disparaître tout à coup comme le démon d'un cauchemar.

Mrs. Stanley mourut: Eliza demeura seule avec son frère, et jeune encore avait été plus d'une fois recherchée en mariage sans pouvoir dire si elle était veuve, et obligée de raconter sa pénible histoire.

APPENDIX

Translation by Sophie Zins

Mrs. Stanley, the mother of Eliza (latterly Mrs. Stanley-Krasinska), had lost her husband a few years before she settled in London with the intention of perfecting the education of her daughter. The girl, who exhibited a remarkable affinity for music, needed to acquire a talent she could use as, aside from a contested inheritance, the widow and her children had no fortune or prospects of obtaining one. One of the sons (she had two) had emigrated to Canada for a government job; the other became a civil servant in the city, and Mrs. Stanley and Eliza had rented a modest house in order to be closer to his office.

It was in October 1813, shortly after the Battle of Leipzig, that young Mr. Stanley made the acquaintance of a Polish officer from the duchy of Posen, who had come to London on leave to recover from his wounds, posing as Blücher's aide-de-camp, and calling himself Count Casimir Krasinski. Soon, young Stanley introduced this foreigner with the charming manners to his mother. Armed with the interest afforded to those courageously outfitted with a sling and a crutch, Casimir Krasinski quickly became intimate with the Stanley household.

Krasinski often came for tea, where he amused his hosts with stories of his campaigns and where he skilfully introduced the subject of his ancestors, mentioning the hope he had of taking possession of their domains, when peace would put everyone back where they belong. He was certain, by the bye, of the protection of his general, as well as that of Frederick William III of Prussia, whom he was proud to serve in defiance of Napoleon.

He would then show a topographic map of his paternal lands, his family tree, letters from Blücher and other pieces in Polish or German that he translated for the Stanley ladies. It had been a month since he had healed, and it was surprising not to see him leave. This was when he declared his intention to settle in England if Miss Stanley agreed to become his wife, a declaration greatly welcomed by the mother, the daughter and the brother, who were all delighted by the charming Polish man.

On the 7th of April 1814, he came exultantly to his wife-to-be and announced the occupation of Paris by the Allies. 'Europe,' he added, 'will change face, and my fortune too – but I have to leave without delay. I have to be with my former general within fifteen days.' Eliza paled at the idea of a separation; Mrs. Stanley shed tears. But Krasinski hastened to reassure her: 'Were I already in possession of my properties,' he said, 'I would believe myself the most cowardly of men if I was ungrateful towards the tender hospitality I have received in London...If I do not keep the oaths that tie me to this family, which I want to make my own – or rather, if I forgot the debt and affection that I owe to you – I would not know how to stifle the pain in my heart. In these circumstance, I am forced to apply to the marriage, which is still my most cherished ambition, one solitary condition: it is that it must be immediate!' Eliza extended her hand with a smile, but Mrs. Stanley was still crying. 'I understand,' said Krasinski. 'You think I want to take your daughter away...No. I say she keeps her mother and that the three of us live in my castle as soon as it is returned to me. I am an orphan and I chose a second mother at the same time as a wife...' Anyway, the chivalrous character of the Polish officer was admired: his generosity was gratefully appreciated; the marriage was hastened; and, after fifteen days, Krasinski drove his new family to Paris. There, at the very dawn of peace, they gathered together with the richest foreigners in a Parisian hotel.

For five days, Krasinski went back and forth between the Prussian army staff and the hotel, bringing news and saying how happy his general was to see him again. Blücher also wanted Mrs. Krasinska and her mother to be introduced to him: the old victor was so paternalistic that he demanded his Aide-de-Camp bring them without any sort of ceremony, without any finery, with their simplest dresses on. 'Thus,' Krasinski told them, 'you are good as you are now. Wait for me this evening and I will come get you once I deliver a message that my general has entrusted to me.' It was while dining, at dessert, that Krasinski talked thus. Left with her mother, his wife waited for his return, both languishing in the dining room until ten, impatient for his return, starting up at the sound of each carriage that stopped in front of the hotel's door. The eleventh hour struck: Krasinski hadn't come back. Midnight: the hotel's guests, strangers to the family, began to arrive back from the soirées or spectacles that they had attended.

All of a sudden, a clamour rose from the stairs and the corridors…Almost simultaneously, everyone noticed there had been a robbery. Each and every apartment had been invaded; every drawer rummaged through; the jewellery and money weren't there anymore. Nothing is faster than suspicion when a thief has taken his spoils.

From one to another, the rumour spread that the thief could only be the Polish count. In the midst of their woe, Mrs. Stanley and her daughter found themselves accused of being the villain's accomplices…The questions and accusations came in a babel of foreign languages. They were asked repeatedly what happened to the man they waited for. Unable to understand, unable to answer, they were troubled and overwhelmed.

Soon a police officer came, called by the plaintiffs. The women saw their room searched and realised they were stripped like the hotel's other inhabitants. They were almost happy about this discovery, which seemed to both absolve the absent and especially prove their innocence. But, on the contrary, this circumstance went against them: it was exclaimed it had been arranged thus to divert suspicion, and suspicion took it out on the two English women. They were arrested; they were put in prison. For two days they hoped in vain that Krasinski, whose disappearance seemed like an enigma to them, would come and say something…

Subsequently, they appeared before the police super-intendent and were acquitted. But they found themselves isolated, foreigners, strangers and still suspects, going in vain to the Prussian army staff to request an audience with General Blücher and mentioning a name that would be a protective talisman for them. They learnt there that the general had never known a Casimir Krasinski nor heard of him.

The women then spoke to the English embassy and saw themselves reduced to accepting the beggarly charity grant-ed to them by the ambassador granted to allow them to return to London beside the young Stanley, who remained the sole support for his mother and sister. For fifteen years, through many sorts of tribulations – poor for a long time, then succeeding in their case on the contested inheritance – Mrs. Stanley and her daughter kept before their eyes the image of this absconded stranger, who, under the guise of romance, had become entwined with their destiny, only to disappear suddenly like a devil from a nightmare.

Mrs. Stanley died; Eliza remained alone with her brother, and, being young still, was more than once sought for marriage, but, being unable to say if she was a widow, declined such offers, obligated at such times to retell her painful story.

ACKNOWLEDGMENTS

The Colonial Australian Popular Fiction series grew out of discussions between the fledgling Grattan Street Press and the Australian Centre about the possibility of reprinting colonial texts. Particular thanks must go to Ken Gelder, who not only contributed his skill and expertise to this book, but who also, from the very beginning, inspired us with his enthusiasm for both the material and the project. Rachael Weaver joined the project soon after those initial discussions: her patience, care and knowledge have been instrumental in enabling us to produce a work of scholarly rigour and excellence. Over and above their contribution to the book, Ken and Rachael have been generous in the time they have given to Grattan Street Press in its infancy. Their passion and excitement for texts in the series have been contagious.

We are grateful also to Sophie Zins, who translated the 'short episode' in French included by Lang in the first edition. *Nous vous remercions!*

Thanks too to the Australian Centre's Amanda Morris, who has given her time and knowledge freely to the press; to Joe Arthur and Ben Kreunen from the University Digitisation Centre, who helped us with the preparation of this work; and to Deborah Lee of Ingram Content Group, whose advice and support has helped us throughout the establishment of the press.

Within the publishing program, many people contributed to the press's development, notably Aaron Mannion, Mark Davis, Matthias Lanz, Beth Driscoll and Sybil Nolan.

We would like to thank our home department, the School of Culture and Communication, in the Faculty of Arts. We are especially grateful for the support of our former Head of School, Rachel Fensham; our acting Head of School, Stephanie Trigg; our school manager, John Boardman; and the Faculty of Arts External Relations team, in particular Fiona Abud, Michelle Kelly and Jessica Pearce. Without the support of the university and our colleagues, Grattan Street Press would not exist.

STAFF ACKNOWLEDGMENTS

Grattan Street Press relies on the talent, enthusiasm and hard work of the students involved. As the subject coordinator, I would like to thank the following students: Jonathon Ball, Anthea Bariamis, Paul Bugeja, Madeleine Charters, Steph Connell, Christine Ebbs, Sarah Farquharson, Lina Hawi, Kat Hunt, Bianca Jafari, Anna James, Melissa Lane, Alex Longmire, Ursula Robinson-Shaw, Claire Shearwood, Ellen Stephens, Hayley Stevenson and Vladana Zivadinovic. I think the future of publishing is in good hands.

Aaron Mannion (Subject Coordinator)

ABOUT GRATTAN STREET PRESS

Grattan Street Press is a trade publisher based in Melbourne. A start-up press, we aim to publish a range of work, including contemporary literature, trade non-fiction, and children's books, and to re-publish culturally valuable works that are out of print. The press is an initiative of the Publishing and Communications program in the School of Culture and Communication at the University of Melbourne, and is staffed by graduate students, who receive hands-on experience of every aspect of the publication process.

The press is a not-for-profit organisation that seeks to build long-term relationships within the Australian literary and publishing community. We also partner with community organisations in Melbourne and beyond to co-publish books that contribute to public knowledge and discussion.

Organisations interested in partnering with us can contact us at coordinator@grattanstreetpress.com.